She went to hit him in a flash of white-hot rage

"Temper, temper," he said softly as he caught her in his arms, clamping her own behind her back. "Did I hit a nerve? You know, one day I'll kiss you when you're soft and compliant."

She was in helpless tears, in fact, when his mouth left hers at last, and it helped not one whit that he held her shaking body close until she regained some composure, before pushing her away.

"Listen, Mel—" she wiped her eyes with the back of her hand "—enough is enough. I'm not what you think I am. I—"

"Oh, I know there's some deep dark mystery there, but, you see, I'm not entirely what you think I am, either."

LINDSAY ARMSTRONG married an accountant from New Zealand and settled down—if you can call it that—in Australia. A coast-to-coast camping trip later, they moved to a six-hundred-acre mixed-grain property, which they eventually abandoned to the mice and leeches and blackflies. Then, after a winning career at the track with an untried trotter, purchased "mainly because he had blue eyes," they opted for a more conventional family life with their five children in Brisbane, where Lindsay now writes.

Books by Lindsay Armstrong

HARLEQUIN PRESENTS
1295—ONE MORE NIGHT
1327—A LOVE AFFAIR
1439—THE DIRECTOR'S WIFE
1487—LEAVE LOVE ALONE
1546—A DANGEROUS LOVER
1569—DARK CAPTOR

HARLEQUIN ROMANCE
2582—PERHAPS LOVE
2653—DON'T CALL IT LOVE
2785—SOME SAY LOVE
2876—THE HEART OF THE MATTER
2893—WHEN THE NIGHT GROWS COLD
3013—THE MARRYING GAME

Don't miss any of our special offers. Write to us at the following address for information on our newest releases.

Harlequin Reader Service
P.O. Box 1397, Buffalo, NY 14240
Canadian address: P.O. Box 603,
Fort Erie, Ont. L2A 5X3

LINDSAY ARMSTRONG

An Unusual Affair

Harlequin Books

TORONTO • NEW YORK • LONDON
AMSTERDAM • PARIS • SYDNEY • HAMBURG
STOCKHOLM • ATHENS • TOKYO • MILAN
MADRID • WARSAW • BUDAPEST • AUCKLAND

Harlequin Presents first edition October 1993
ISBN 0-373-11593-8

Original hardcover edition published in 1991
by Mills & Boon Limited

AN UNUSUAL AFFAIR

CHAPTER ONE

'DARLING, you look dreadful, you've told me you're not exactly flush and that you need a good few months of peace and quiet to get this thesis written that you rushed about Africa assembling—what could be better than for you to stay in this little place of mine which will be absolutely empty otherwise? And anyway, you are my favourite niece!'

'I'm your only niece,' Rachel replied, but affectionately, 'and you're right, I do look dreadful.' She ran her hands through her long dark hair, which was dry and lifeless, and grimaced down at her crumpled jeans. 'Mind you, I have just got off a plane after flying for *days*, but I wouldn't be at all surprised if people took *me* for *your* aunt instead of the other way around.'

Samantha Soldido smiled. In fact, she was only ten years older than her niece, having been much younger than Rachel's father, her only brother, and, at thirty-eight to Rachel's twenty-eight, she still had a girlish figure and considerable if somewhat flamboyant style. The reason for this was twofold: she'd never had any children, and she'd married an elderly Italian millionaire, now deceased, who had left her more money than she could spend in one lifetime, although that didn't stop her trying.

'Here we are—at least have a look at it,' she pleaded, and brought her Mercedes coupé to a less than smooth halt.

'But I don't understand,' Rachel said, climbing wearily out and glancing up at the two-storeyed terraced house in an old but fashionable inner city suburb of Sydney. 'Did Guido—was this one of his investments? You never lived here, did you?' she added, picturing her aunt's mansion on the North Shore.

'Not exactly,' Samantha murmured. 'Come in.'

Ten minutes later, Rachel said in somewhat dazed tones, 'Sam, what is this?' She stared at the painting of a voluptuous nude that dominated the hall. 'It looks just like a love-nest— Sam,' she rounded on her aunt, 'you didn't!'

'Well, I did,' her aunt replied with a shrug.

'Did Guido *know*?'

'Not exactly, but you must remember that for the last few years of his life Guido was——' she gestured delicately '—and so long as I provided him with companionship and support—which I did, Rachel, I was very attached to Guido—I'm sure he didn't expect me to go without ... things, nor would he have wanted to be bothered with the details.'

'Then he must have been a very understanding man, Sam,' Rachel said with some irony as she wandered through the main downstairs room that could only be adequately described as a *salon*, she felt. There were yellow-velvet-covered settees and drapes, marble pedestals topped with statuary, crystal objects and lamps—she remembered wryly that one of Guido's businesses had been importing marble from Italy—an ornate marble fireplace, some beautiful paintings and the finest Samarkand carpet she'd ever seen, complete with cloud bands, pomegranate, lotus and peony in yellow, blue and lacquer-red. She wasn't sure, she decided, which was the more spectacular room, this or the main bedroom that was completely done in blue and silver. It wasn't a large house; there was a second bedroom upstairs which had so far escaped Sam's attentions, a dining-room downstairs which hadn't, but also a rather nice colonial kitchen with a breakfast-nook that looked through french doors out on to a minute tiled courtyard planted with flowering shrubs and lemon trees in tubs. All the same...

'Sam, you're very sweet——' Rachel turned to her aunt '—but this house just isn't me.'

Samantha Soldido's still beautiful blue eyes took on a look her husband Guido had come to know well. 'Perhaps it's time for a change, then,' she remarked. 'Anyway, does it matter just for a few months? At least you'll be comfortable, and you'd be doing me a favour. Keeping an eye on it, that kind of thing.'

Rachel narrowed her own rather remarkable blue eyes. 'Are you going somewhere?'

'I'm going overseas for a while. It's so unfortunate that you've come home just as I'm about to leave, but you didn't give me much warning,' she said reproachfully.

'I know; sorry. Are you going on your own?'

'No.' Sam grinned. 'Well, I'm going on my own, but I won't be on my own when I get there. I don't enjoy being on my own.'

'What about the North Shore——?'

'It's on the market. It's far too big for me.'

'Well...' Rachel looked around, and it crossed her mind that it would solve a lot of problems.

'Oh, do it, Rachel,' Sam entreated. 'I really don't know why you have to be so stiff-necked about everything I offer you! I'm your only living close relative.'

'That doesn't mean I have to sponge off you,' Rachel replied with a grin.

'When have you ever done that?' her aunt asked with that dangerous look in her eye. 'You've refused every little thing I've tried to do for you—don't you understand that, when one is in the position to be Lady Bountiful, it's *very* frustrating when you're not allowed to? Besides, I feel some responsibility for you.'

'There's really no need——'

'There is,' Sam said in a very genuinely frustrated way. 'Aren't we part of the same mad family? You have to admit, the way your mother and father carted you all over the world when you were little—even allowed you to be born in some rotten, flea-ridden tent in Morocco—was quite mad! Then they had to get themselves killed in an earthquake in some other godforsaken part of the world they had no right to even be in, considering they had a daughter... How much of your life did you spend in boarding-schools wherever they decided to dump you? Years,' she said with passion.

'Yes, but it wasn't your fault,' Rachel pointed out.

'Well,' Sam grimaced. 'I should have at least offered to take you—they probably wouldn't have agreed but...' She shrugged. Then she said rather soberly, 'Rachel, to tell you the truth, it's lately dawned on me that I have a lot of money but not much else. Approaching forty makes you think about these things.' She smiled wryly. 'I don't say I would have done things any differently, but I do now value those things I can't buy. You're one of the few of them. It would make me very happy to do *something* for you; it would make me feel that I'm not absolutely alone in the world.'

'Sam, darling, so long as I'm around, you aren't, and I never meant to make you feel like that——'

'Then indulge me in this, which is nothing really!'

'All right, but——'

'Oh, marvellous!' Sam clapped her hands. 'Why don't you move in right away? I'll spend the couple of days before I go with you and— and don't you dare argue—I shall take you to my beautician tomorrow, who is a genius, because you sure as hell need it!'

Rachel laughed. 'Actually, I love the sound of it. But don't you need to collect *your* things?'

'Dear Rachel,' Sam replied patiently, 'what is the use of a love-nest if it's not fully equipped? I keep an extensive wardrobe here, all my favour- ite cosmetics—by the way, we're the same size, so feel free——'

'Sam, no, not your clothes too,' Rachel objected.

'From the look of that single battered suitcase you arrived with, pet, you're going to need them.'

'But——'

'Rachel!'

'Well, only until I get some others.'

'We'll see,' Sam murmured.

'All off!'

Rachel frowned at her reflection in the ornate mirror and that of the slightly demented-looking little man standing beside her with her aunt hovering behind him. 'All?' she said doubtfully.

'But of course.' Mr Leon waved his arms. 'With the bone-structure——' he curved his hands down Rachel's face '—with the *eyes*, the body— these square shoulders and lean lines, I can make you look austere, yet hint that you're not austere at all underneath.' He gazed at Rachel, clad in one of Sam's exquisitely plain white linen shirts. 'Ah, quite tantalising, yes. You will drive men wild,' he finished simply.

'Well...'

'Besides——' Mr Leon gingerly lifted a tress of hair '—it's like straw. What do you think, Mrs Soldido?'

'I think yes. I told you he was a genius, Rachel,' Sam said with a glint of excitement in her eye. 'What's wrong?'

'I'm not into driving men wild—assuming you're right——'

'Then it's about time you were. Do it, Leon!' Sam commanded. 'Really, Rachel,' she added, 'it's far more practical for the odd things you spend your life doing, anyway. Why didn't you get it cut over there instead of letting it get like this?'

'Where I was they did other things with their hair,' Rachel said ruefully. 'Such as beading it and packing it with pig grease and mud. Oh, go ahead!'

'How do you feel?'

Rachel grimaced. 'Exhausted.' They were eating dinner in the kitchen. It had been an exhausting day. Not only had her crowning glory been shorn into a boyish cap, but she'd been sauna'd, massaged, mudpacked, oil-treated, manicured and pedicured and taught how to apply make-up to make the very best of her bone-structure and eyes. Mr Leon, who could apparently turn his hands to anything, had even given her a lecture on the style of clothes she should wear, and Sam had raided her wardrobe and come up with them.

'You know, he's right,' Sam said now as she lifted a succulent piece of cucumber from the salad, 'You will drive men wild if you don't let yourself go again. Why are you so determinedly not into it?'

Rachel ate silently for a moment. Then she sipped her wine and said thoughtfully, 'I don't think I'm cut out for marriage. My mad father, who was also your mad brother, left me with his genes, I'm afraid. A genuine wanderlust.'

'Well, but he found someone to go along with it. Your equally mad mother.' Sam grinned.

'Do you know,' Rachel twirled her wine glass, 'despite women's liberation, it's still not so easy to organise things the other way round? I mean, men may be able to drag their wives around, but they're still not too amenable to being dragged around themselves, or left alone for long periods of time. Strange, isn't it? Or is it just that there are some things you can never change.'

Sam made a moue over her prawns. 'I take it there have been involvements, then?'

'Yes, two,' Rachel replied.

'And you're very bitter now?'

'No.' Rachel smiled absently. 'I'd go mad tied to a kitchen sink.'

'Wary, then,' Sam said.

'Yes.'

'Mmm.'

Rachel narrowed her eyes at her aunt. 'Sam—look, I appreciate all this, I really do, but don't—don't you dare try your hand at organising my love-life.'

Her aunt looked a picture of injured innocence. But she said. 'One ball was all I had in mind. How could that possibly be——?'

'No.'

'It's tomorrow night. It's a charity ball for a children's hospital; the cream of Sydney society will be there; I am on the organising committee, and—to be perfectly honest, my party is one female short.'

Rachel closed her eyes. 'Not a blind date, Sam!'

Sam laughed. 'Hardly—he's sixty if he's a day and still mourning the loss of his wife—but he's a very nice man and could be willing to cough up a lot of dough. And you don't have to *partner* him, just even up the numbers.'

'Why don't you all just cough up your dough and have done with it?' Rachel enquired with some impatience.

'Because this way is much more fun—you'll see!'

'No—I'm not coming.'

But she went.

'Rachel, you look stunning.'

Sam stared at her niece, who was wearing a fitted, strapless black gown that was elegantly simple and glittered as she moved, and long black gloves. Truth to tell, Rachel barely recognised herself. Mr Leon's expertise had transformed her into a cool, glamorous creature, and the only slight giveaway might have been the rather wry look in her smoky blue eyes, which had been transformed from beautiful to stunning with artful eye make-up. The gloves hid her hands, which had been in the same state as her hair and not as easily reclaimable.

'Just one thing—this,' Sam said triumphantly, and put on a chunky silver necklace and slid a matching bracelet over one glove. 'There.' She herself glowed in bouffant blue silk. 'Now remember, enjoy yourself,' she commanded.

'I'll try. So long as *you* remember this is your last chance to play Lady Bountiful.'

'I'll be perfectly content now,' Sam assured her. 'I'll know you're comfortable and able to do your thesis without having to eat the flies off the wall. And I'll know I've at least introduced you

to Sydney society—after all, what do they say
about acorns and oak trees?' she winked at
Rachel.

'You're incorrigible,' Rachel declared, with not
the slightest premonition.

Unfortunately—and she couldn't believe Sam had
engineered it this way—the sixty-year old
widower took one look at her and all thoughts
of his recent bereavement fled his mind.

He manoeuvred himself to sit next to her, he
plied her with champagne and because he was
quite knowledgeable about Africa, he engaged
her in interesting conversation for quite a time
before she realised that he was acting rather
strangely for a man who had not long lost his
wife.

Then she sent a distress signal out to Sam, who
took her away briefly and laughed fit to kill
herself. 'I told you!'

'But——'

'It's not only him, darling, although I really
wouldn't have suspected him of it, which just goes
to show! But I'll introduce you to some of the
others who are panting to meet you.'

'No——'

But Sam ignored her and bore her relentlessly
across to another table. It didn't work for long.
Her elderly admirer followed her, and for the next
couple of hours wherever she turned, there he
was, exhibiting an unmistakable air of
possessiveness.

To make matters worse, she closed her eyes in
silent irritation once, and upon opening them

found herself staring into the mocking grey eyes of a strange man who then let his gaze drift leisurely over her and strip her naked, take in her hovering companion and come back to clash with her gaze in a way that left her in no doubt of what he thought.

'Who—who is that man over there?' Rachel heard herself asking a female member of Sam's party a few minutes later—heard herself with a kind of disbelief.

'Which one?'

'He's got—grey eyes and dark hair——'

'Oh, darling, that's Mel Carlisle. Isn't he gorgeous?'

'Well—but who is he?'

'Don't you know? Of course, you've been away. He's a very brilliant orthopaedic surgeon, and so young. Well, to be a surgeon. I think he's only about thirty-five, and unmarried, although not necessarily unattached—are they ever?' she said with a sigh. 'I believe he's going to give a speech. He does a lot of work at our hospital.'

Mel Carlisle did indeed give a speech, which demonstrated that he was not only good with bones but good with words, and good-looking in a tall, dark way that set most of the women watching him drooling. His speech wasn't long, was witty in parts and then quite moving when he got on to the subject of the deformed children they could all help.

The audience responded enthusiastically; he was stopped many times on the way back to his table, and Rachel tensed and waited for the inevitable. It didn't happen. Even Sam looked briefly bemused as he sidestepped her table—which was, after all, one of the committee tables, and the only one he missed—and finally sat down at his own. But to Rachel it seemed to be an extremely pointed gesture, and this was confirmed when their gazes caught again after he sat down and the mockery in his eyes hadn't changed.

Who does he think he is? she thought with a sudden little pang of anger; and to show that she didn't give a damn she raised her champagne glass to him in an ironic little salute, and turned pointedly back to her elderly admirer.

'Rachel, I am sorry about last night.'

'Sam, you're forgiven!' Rachel stretched and yawned. It was ten o'clock but she was still wearing one of Sam's gorgeous silk wrappers and was finding it curiously hard to get going. Sam, looking exotic as only blondes could in jungle-green and with a lot of gold jewellery, was on the point of going herself.

'Now, we've covered everything, haven't we?' Her aunt's practical side had been asserting itself this morning. Keys, rubbish collections, the cleaning lady who came in once a week, all had been covered.

'Everything,' Rachel said with another yawn. 'I drank too much champagne last night,' she added ruefully. 'Er—what about the neighbours? Do they know you?'

'Hardly,' Sam said with a unrepentant grin. 'Well, except the old biddy across the road. I suspect she sits behind her lace curtains all day. And the house next door,' she pointed, 'was recently sold. No idea who to or when they'll move in, but they must have a bit of brass. Values have soared here. It's quite an ''in'' place to live, Rachel.'

'I believe you,' Rachel murmured. 'Why won't you let me come to the airport?'

Sam frowned briefly. 'It might be embarrassing, darling.'

'Oh? Sam,' she said slowly, 'this trip is not a case of ''off with the old, on with the new''?'

'Exactly.'

'You really are——'

'I know,' Sam said. 'When I'm forty I'll reform.' She bent and kissed her niece. 'Now don't work too hard!'

Rachel didn't work at all on her thesis that day. She spent most of it organising the second bedroom as a study, did some food and stationery shopping, noted the furniture van outside the house next door with the lift of an eyebrow, and sorted through her clothes before deciding gloomily that not even a charity shop would be interested in them. She also spent some time pondering why she felt oddly dull and telling herself that, after months of basic rations, she'd plunged into wining and dining a little too richly—it had to be that. It surely couldn't have anything to do with a certain orthopaedic surgeon and his insolent deductions.

All the same, as she sat eating a lonely and very plain evening meal, she found herself thinking of him again and wondering what kind of women he liked and how, for example, he would react to her true self.

It was while she wondering this that she saw a streak of feline grey cross the courtyard and by way of a marble table leap on to the wall dividing Sam's back garden from the house that had been moved into during the day. It sat on top of the wall washing its face, then looking around regally before disappearing over the other side.

Rachel smiled. She had no affinity with cats, but admired their independence and, thinking of it, reflected that she should be counting her blessings instead of feeling deflated. After all, she passionately wanted her doctorate in agricultural economics, and Sam's offer of this rent-free accommodation meant that she could attack her thesis wholeheartedly, whereas without it she would have had to find a part-time job to augment the small amount of money her parents had left her—small *and* dwindling. Moreover, perhaps a bit of luxury wouldn't hurt her; it *had* been a long, hard grind this far.

So thinking, she took herself upstairs to the fantastic silver and blue bathroom, where she had a spa bath, and once more anointed herself with one of Sam's beautifully perfumed body lotions. Then she draped herself again in the blue silk robe with love-birds embroidered on it in silver thread and took herself downstairs to the *salon* to explore the state-of-the-art record player hidden behind an exotic screen.

And she was relaxing on one of the yellow settees, sipping Malaysian Cameronian tea and drinking in Bach through her pores, when the doorbell rang.

She sat up and frowned, then shrugged.

It was Mel Carlisle standing on the doorstep, with an angry grey Persian cat anchored under his arm.

'Sorry to bother you, but I wondered if this was your cat,' he said, and stopped, his grey eyes narrowing. 'Well, well,' he added then with irony. 'Fancy running into you again. How do you do? I moved in next door today.'

Rachel's jaw dropped and the cat, with a dexterous twist of its body, took advantage of the pause to gain its freedom and vent its rage at the same time. It leapt from its captor to Rachel, who caught it in a reflex action, got scratched for her pains and relegated as, with another astonishing bound, the creature streaked into the *salon*, climbed a marble pedestal, and knocked a china figurine off it, which bounced on to the table where Rachel's tea was, smashing the cup, and itself. The cat sat down atop the pedestal and smoothed its whiskers.

Rachel flew in after it with a muttered curse, then turned and said roundly, 'No, it is not my cat, and that figurine was probably Meissen and the cup and saucer I know for a fact were—what's wrong?'

Mel Carlisle didn't answer for a moment as he gazed around with his hands shoved in his pockets, then he whistled softly and looked at Rachel. 'Is this what I think it is?'

'*What* do you think it is?' she asked coldly.

'Well,' he said softly, dropping his gaze to the outline of her breasts beneath the thin blue silk, 'it crossed my mind last night that you might be a high-class hooker, but this is even higher than I had in mind.' He grinned crookedly. 'Where's your—er—patron? Has he gone back to his wife for the night?'

Rachel was not sure what she would have answered, because the doorbell rang and the cat dived off the pillar and hid behind a chair. 'Just don't touch him,' she said through her teeth, and brushed past him as the bell rang again.

There was a cheerful young man dressed in a chauffeur livery on the doorstep this time, and in his hand was a set of car keys.

'Who——?' Rachel began, then glanced past him at the car parked at the kerb—Sam's dark blue Mercedes coupé and another car behind it with its parking lights on. She closed her eyes. Sam had offered her the Mercedes but she had refused resolutely, and her aunt had backed down with nothing more than a thoughtful look. *I should have known*, Rachel raged. She opened her eyes. 'Look——'

But the cheerful young man said brightly, 'I was told to tell you, ma'am, that the car is for your exclusive use, and to give you this.' He handed Rachel the keys and a slip of paper. 'It's a petrol account, ma'am, with the garage around the corner,' he confided. 'They'll take care of any problems you might have with it, too. Though you shouldn't; it's a real beauty! They also have parking there should you need it. Goodnight, ma'am.' He touched his cap.

'Wait,' Rachel began but he'd been well coached. He backed down the path, smiling widely at her, and jumped into the second car, which drove off.

Rachel closed the door and leant back against it, then realised that Mel Carlisle was watching her and that he must have heard and seen the lot—which for a man with a suspicious mind anyway would probably only be read one way. 'I can explain,' she said jaggedly.

'You don't have to—why on earth should you?' He raised a dark eyebrow at her. 'We're only neighbours, after all. Although,' he paused thoughtfully, 'I can't help wondering how long all this, and fancy cars et cetera, will compensate for the kind of serious frustration you were feeling last night. Are you ever allowed a young lover just to...let off steam? Dance with, say, and not worry if he's going to have a heart attack on you, let alone die in bed with you? It must be a problem.'

Rachel took a very deep breath and, despite the flash of anger in her eyes, couldn't for the life of her prevent herself from saying coolly, 'Oh, I go away to do that. I do have a few principles, you know, and one of them involves not sharing one man's bed with someone else, so if you're thinking of applying for the position think again.'

'There's always my bed,' he replied lazily. 'In fact it's brand-new and unslept-in yet, so I haven't shared it with anyone, and just think how handy it would be. I'm sure we could fix up a way to cross our mutual wall at the back so no one would even see you coming and going.'

Rachel clenched her fists behind her back. 'You overrate yourself, Mr Carlisle. *I* choose who I sleep with——'

'When you don't get paid for it, do you mean?' he shot back, then grinned his crooked grin when she flushed with anger. But why the hell am I angry? Rachel asked herself—and immediately told herself precisely why. Because this man had so profoundly misjudged her, on appearances alone—well, she conceded, perhaps appearances had contrived to be misleading, but all the same— and, on top of it, here he was asking her to sleep with him, which made him as bad as he thought she was if not a lot worse. She was damned, suddenly, if she wasn't going to play this out to the hilt, then have the marvellous satisfaction of rubbing his face in what she really was.

'Oh, well,' she murmured with a shrug, and pushed herself away from the door. 'I guess we all earn our livings at what we're best at. And, seeing as you can't choose your neighbours and we're stuck with each other, providing you don't make any more propositions, because I really couldn't—next door is still a bit too close to home—I don't see why we shouldn't...be amiable. Would you like a drink while we sort out how to deal with this impossible cat?'

CHAPTER TWO

MEL CARLISLE took the glass of brandy Rachel offered him—she hadn't waited for a reply but sauntered past him and poured two drinks—with a rather quizzical look. 'Are you allowed to do this?'

Rachel shrugged delicately and said, while she carefully collected bits of Meissen figurine and teacup and mopped tea off the carpet, 'Don't worry, he's not liable to burst in and shoot you or anything dramatic; he's overseas for six weeks. Do sit down. Where's the cat?' She bent over the back of the chair it had disappeared behind and rose up with a grin. 'Sound asleep, would you believe?' She curled up in a corner of the settee with her drink. 'Cheers. Welcome to the neighbourhood.'

'Thank you.' He sat down and cradled the balloon glass in his long lands. 'Why aren't you overseas with him—incidentally, since we're neighbours and might have cause to refer to him frequently, does he have a name?'

Rachel considered. 'You can call him Joe, which is not his real name, of course.'

'Of course. Why aren't you?'

Rachel grimaced. 'He took his wife. By the way——' it crossed her mind that she could be seriously slandering a certain widower who was not overseas anyway, and didn't have a wife, but all the same '—that wasn't Joe last night.' She stopped and realised she might have led herself into an awkward bit of explaining...

'Ah.' Mel Carlisle thought for a while, then said, 'Another contender for your services, was he? I guess you have to keep your options open in this...ancient profession.'

Rachel controlled a sudden urge to rise and slap his face, despite the fact that he'd unwittingly come up with a better explanation than she might have provided if pressed.

She said instead with another shrug. 'Perhaps.' Then she smiled gently. 'Has the neighbourhood suddenly lost a bit of *ton* since you discovered what this is?' she queried, and added, 'It could be worse—you know, streams of strange men.' She gestured wryly.

He lay back and studied her. 'Do you also mean *you* could be worse?'

'Well, I suppose I could,' she mused. 'One steady man is a bit like one steady job, isn't it?'

'Have you never had any ambition to do anything else with your life?'

'Oh, one day. It's rather difficult when you have expensive tastes, you see.'

'I see.' He drank some brandy then reached for the sleeve of the Bach album, and shot her a narrowed grey look.

Rachel ran a hand through her short hair and laid her head back. 'You know, all this doesn't mean to say I can't be a cultured, reasonably intelligent person.'

'I've heard that argument too,' he commented. 'Put along the lines of—it's my body and if I want to sell it who should tell me not to? And I've no doubt there've been many women with little option and I suppose, if it's a way to survive, who does? But to consciously make it a way of life...' He didn't go on.

Rachel sighed. 'Is about as low as any woman can go? For all you know, Mr Carlisle—or should I call you Doctor?'

'Call me Mel. What do I call you?'

'Well apart from Scarlet or Fallen or anything more direct, my name is Rachel Wright. But for all you know, Mel, Joe might be young and vigorous, tied to an unfortunate marriage, say, and I might be deeply in love with him. Who then would earn most of your contempt, him or me?'

'I think I'd divide it equally,' Mel Carlisle mused. 'Assuming I believed it.'

'Why wouldn't you?'

'Well, young, vigorous men don't generally need to go to these lengths, especially not with someone deeply in love with them.' He glanced around and shook his head in some disbelief. 'And I don't think you'd have got as angry as you did at the mention of *young* lovers just now, or as irritated to death with elderly ones as you looked last night, if it were true.'

'I see.'

'So I'm right?' He looked at her with sardonic amusement.

Rachel stared at her glass then shrugged— something she was learning to do with a variety of nuances. 'What's it to you, anyway?' she murmured. 'You don't for one minute assume that moving in next door to me gives you the slightest right to tell me how to live my life, do you?'

'Not at all, Rachel,' he said blandly. 'Let's call it an exchange of views. Surely intelligent, cultured people can do that?'

'There's a difference between being clever with people's bones and being intelligent in a more universal and understanding sense. In fact, being clever with people's bones doesn't at all mean to say you're not an insensitive boor. All it really says to me so far is that you have a holier-than-thou attitude I find—a *crashing* bore.' Good God, she thought as she sat up impatiently, anyone would think I'd studied for the part! 'What are we going to do about this wretched cat?'

'I've no idea. He's been wandering around my place tripping me up for hours.'

'Well, if he lives around here, you'd think he'd have gone home, wouldn't you?' Rachel said slowly. 'After investigating you, I mean.'

'That's what I thought. Until I put him outside for about the sixth time and in he came every time I opened the back door. There's no one home on the other side of me and, to be perfectly honest, I don't feel like doing a lengthy door-knock with a hostile cat. You wouldn't consider keeping him for the night now he's settled down, would you? We could ring up the RSPCA in the morning if no one comes looking for *him*.'

Rachel grimaced. 'I suppose I could. He's probably quite valuable, but anyway, someone might love him. Any more damages, though,' she warned, 'and he's straight back to you. You were his first choice, after all.'

'Don't you like cats?' Mel Carlisle enquired.

'I prefer to admire them from a distance.'

'Do you, now?' He was silent for a moment, staring at his drink, and Rachel took the opportunity to study him and decide that in serviceable khaki trousers and an open-necked green and blue checked shirt with dusty marks on it, and with his thick dark hair ruffled, he didn't look like a dedicated surgeon, although none of it altered the fact that he was proportioned rather like a Greek god with wide shoulders and slim hips, long legs and beautiful hands. And has a clever, insulting way with words, she reminded herself, and was slightly startled to find that he was now returning her stare. He also said, 'I guess that's what I'll be doing to you now.'

'What?' she asked, looking confused.

'Admiring you from afar,' he murmured with that mocking glint in his eyes.

Which helped Rachel to raise an incredulous eyebrow. 'Oh, come, now!' she said with gentle irony. 'Since your worst suspicions about me have been thoroughly confirmed, you don't expect me to believe——' She stopped rather abruptly.

'That I could be attracted to you, Rachel?' he supplied lazily. 'Oddly enough, one's morals don't seem to dictate who attracts one physically. They can certainly tell you *why* you shouldn't be attracted, but that's about all the say they have in the matter—hadn't you noticed?'

Rachel took refuge in the last of her brandy, then lifted her head to say, with a glint of amusement that surprised her, 'You don't think it's just a time-honoured ambivalence men are very susceptible to, Mel?'

'Such as?'

'Such as while they vocally condemn women like me, they can't help feeling, at the same time, that we're fair game?'

'Ah, well,' he said slowly, 'you might be right. There could certainly be an element of that in it. It would be interesting to know why you, when you market yourself commercially, so to speak, *feel* you should have protection against—free trade. I'm quite sure, Rachel,' he said softly, 'we could have a very interesting discussion about that.' He stood up. 'Unfortunately, moving is an exhausting business, so I'll have to postpone that one——'

'Don't bother!' She was on her feet in a flash and her eyes were cold and angry. 'I'll tell you now. Even in a free-trade situation I have a perfect right to trade as I like. And even if it were a question of going bankrupt, I would do it rather than trade *anything* with you.'

'Well, my dear,' he said rather drily, and Rachel was suddenly conscious of how tall he was, and that, despite her aspersions, it was impossible to deny that he was a dangerously clever opponent in this war of words, 'then we'll be able to talk about things one can't regulate the way one can free trade. Things such as why you even noticed me last night, and why my contempt bothered you enough to retaliate, using a man who wasn't even Joe,' he said with a combination of ingenuousness and derision that was singeing.

'Oh, come on!' Rachel said frustratedly. 'Nearly every woman there was...making a meal of you! You just have those looks, but rest assured that until you stripped me naked——'

He laughed. 'You were the one exception? I don't know about my kind of looks, but last night you were certainly worthy of stripping naked.'

'Because...because...' Rachel was so incensed that she couldn't go on.

'Possibly because you're not the usual run of...what you are,' he said thoughtfully. 'As a matter of fact, my first impression was that you had a kind of class. Of course, I was right. You're obviously very classy—in a certain sense, and Joe obviously appreciates that!' He looked around again. 'But to get back to—well, basics is a good way of putting it. You can deny it until you're blue in the face, Rachel Wright, but there was an instantaneous charge of some kind between us last night, the kind that's ungovernable by things like commerce and trade, morals, et cetera. I'll come over in the morning about the cat. Don't bother to see me out,' he added.

At two o'clock in the morning, Rachel sat up in Sam's bed with silver satin sheets twisted about her and longed for the feel of cool cotton on her skin. She also knew she was having trouble sleeping because Mel Carlisle had been right, damn him, but that didn't mean he would be the kind of man who would understand her; in fact she was quite sure that, if he didn't have a demanding enough career to need a very conventional wife when he chose one, his ego would anyway. Any man who was as uncompromisingly scathing about whores but admitted to seeing them as fair game would have to have a monumental ego, she reasoned. Then she asked herself rather bleakly why she had taken up the cudgels *so* energetically on behalf of whoredom herself when it was about as alien to her nature as anything could be—and decided that most of it *was* a desire to teach Dr Carlisle not to make snap judgements, but that a small part of it was also a defence of her sex. A feeling, even more, that everyone deserved to be judged as individuals, with a history perhaps that had moulded them as much as any other individual was moulded.

She lay back, grimacing. 'What I should really do, though,' she said to herself, 'is put an end to this whole ridiculous thing—I will, first thing in the morning.'

First thing in the morning, after dressing in a pair of Sam's fashionably baggy slate trousers and a wide-shouldered ivory linen shirt tucked in at her narrow waist, she fed the Persian cat some milk and let it out.

It stalked around the courtyard briefly then re-entered the kitchen and leapt on to the draining-board beside the sink, where it sat and stared out of the window like a fluffy Sphinx.

'Yes, well,' Rachel murmured, 'don't imagine I've adopted you, although I assure you I'll do the decent thing and make every effort to see you find your home again. And that,' she said as the doorbell rang, 'is no doubt the good doctor from next door. Is he ever in for a surprise! Stay there for the time being.' She closed the cat into the kitchen and went to answer the door.

It wasn't the doctor but an imperious old lady with snowy white hair in a bun and wearing an old-fashioned selection of scarves, beads and antique rings.

'Hello,' Rachel said politely as she was surveyed with unmistakable hauteur. 'Is there something I can do for you?'

The old lady snorted. 'Never,' she declared, taking Rachel aback somewhat. 'So you're the new one?' she continued. 'Gone for someone younger this time, has he? But I'll tell you something——' she pointed dramatically at the Mercedes still parked at the kerb '—don't think he bought that specially for you! Your predecessor had it.'

'Uh? Oh!' Rachel said as enlightenment dawned. 'No, that was my——'

'Now, don't you try and fob me off with stories, young lady,' the old woman admonished sternly. 'I live opposite, so I know all about the goings-on in this house!'

'I see,' Rachel said slowly, and fought a desire to laugh at the same time as she cursed her aunt still winging her way overseas. 'Well,' she said somewhat helplessly, and wondered how to even begin to explain—which lost her the opportunity.

'The only reason I'm darkening your doorstep is because a few days ago,' the old lady went on, 'I had a funny spell in a shopping centre and they carted me off to hospital and nobody would listen when I tried to tell them about my cat! Now he's gone.' Tears gathered in those accusing, indignant eyes.

'Look,' Rachel said hastily, 'if he's pale grey and Persian, he's here. I'll go and get him.' But all she had to do was open the kitchen door and the cat streaked out, through the house and into the arms of its mistress. But the delighted reunion that then ensued was cut off abruptly. 'At least you had the decency to look after him,' her opposite neighbour said grudgingly, 'I'll give you that. But that doesn't alter the fact that it's the likes of you who can give a neighbourhood a bad name. Good day to you.' She turned away determinedly.

'And good day to you,' Rachel said with a sigh.

Back in the kitchen, she made some raisin toast and coffee for breakfast and was sitting in the breakfast-nook, eating thoughtfully, when there was a clatter on the other side of the wall, then Mel Carlisle appeared on top of it and, using the same marble table the cat had, descended into her courtyard.

'What the hell do you think you're doing?' Rachel demanded angrily as they met at the french door.

'Just protecting my reputation—good morning, Rachel,' he replied.

'Good morning, nothing! What—do you mean?'

'Well, in view of the fact that darkening your doorstep could not only give the neighbourhood a bad name but me one as well, I decided that if I wanted to see you this was the best way to go about it—the most *discreet* anyway.'

'Darkening—you *heard*!'

'Every word,' he agreed. 'I had just opened my bedroom window, which overlooks the street not far from your front door, and *voilà*, as they say. It's a problem with these terraced houses, probably. So Joe traded his old model in for a younger one—I thought you were rather restrained with the old biddy.'

'You——' Rachel struggled for words. 'You are the most two-faced bastard it has ever been my misfortune to meet,' she got out at last. 'What do you think you're doing now?' she spat at him as he put his hands about her waist and lifted her off her feet, so that he could move inside and set her down again.

'I'm being seduced by the marvellous aroma of your coffee,' he said with a grin. 'I have coffee but nothing to make it in, I have a tin of baked beans but nothing to open it with—I was hoping you'd take pity on me and offer me some breakfast. I do like your kitchen, by the way.' He pulled out a chair and sat down.

Rachel stared at him with her hands on her hips, her breasts heaving and her emotions impossible to describe beyond a burgeoning desire to punish him in perhaps the only way she could, a desire that gained the upper hand and quite nullified her intention to be truthful this morning.

She removed her hands from her hips and tossed her head. 'It's not mine, as you very well know. None of it is.' She reached up for another cup and poured him coffee. 'I have fruit and raisin toast for breakfast, that's all.'

'Is that how you keep so fashionably slender? Thank you.' He accepted the coffee. 'By the way, I'm rather glad to know the rest of it wasn't your doing. Your predecessor?' he enquired delicately.

'I have no idea,' Rachel said demurely, then, before she could help herself, added, 'You should see the bedroom.'

He laughed. 'I can imagine.'

'That wasn't an invitation incidentally,' she remarked casting him a suddenly cool look as she toasted raisin bread.

'Of course not. Perish the thought,' he replied gravely.

'Here you are.' She put the toast in front of him and picked out an apple from the fruit bowl. 'I suppose I could always ask—Joe—if I could tone things down a bit at least.'

'Why not ask him if you could redecorate completely? Isn't that a new mistress's prerogative?'

'I might just do that.' She started to peel the apple but, after watching her efforts for a moment, he took it out of her hand and completed the process with the precision of a surgeon.

'Oh,' she said, staring at the perfect coil of peel, 'I never manage to do it like that.'

'Each to his own talent.' He handed her back the apple, then frowned as he looked at her hand. 'You don't have the hands of a . . .' He paused.

'Mistress?'

'I was going to say a lady of leisure.' He lifted his eyes to her face.

'They will be soon. Eat your toast before it gets cold.'

'Yes, ma'am.' But he didn't. 'If this is a fairly new arrangement, I'm surprised Joe could bear to leave you.'

'Joe's time is not always his own,' Rachel said slowly. 'I understand,' she added.

'But if that's the case and he's... reserved the exclusive use of you, Rachel, won't you go round the bend doing nothing most of your life?'

'Who says I'll be doing nothing?' Rachel smiled slightly. 'I am allowed to go out, you know. It's also a fairly time-consuming business to—er—look like this. I can spend the whole day getting my hair cut, my nails done, having a massage. Then there are clothes—and, now you've put me in mind of it, months of fun to be had redecorating this place.'

'I don't believe it,' he said abruptly.

'You believe a lot of other things about me.' She couldn't resist that.

'Well, you just look and sound too intelligent for it. Despite what I might have implied last night.'

She cast him a sardonic look, then she thought for a moment and perceived a way to go. 'An intelligent mistress? As a matter of fact I am, much as you find it incredible. I'm studying for a degree—with Joe's approval. I think he perceives it as rather a cachet, actually, to have an intellectual mistress.'

'What kind of degree?'

'Agricultural economics—look, you came here asking for breakfast; now you won't eat it.'

He looked down at his toast. 'It's a habit from my intern days. I actually prefer some things cold and soggy now.' He ate half a slice. 'Do you go to lectures?'

'At the moment I'm doing it by correspondence.'

'I see.' He finished his toast and reached for an orange.

'You say that,' Rachel mused, 'as if there's no point to it. But you're the one——'

'I'm just wondering what use a degree in agricultural economics is going to be to you. I mean, as a career it has its limitations, even if you were really serious about it.'

'You forget,' Rachel said smoothly, 'this is my career.' She gestured around. 'But I don't think the accumulation of knowledge can ever be entirely useless.'

'Is Joe interested in agricultural economics?'

'Not in the slightest,' Rachel murmured, and proceeded to put the boot in. 'Joe—has lots of good points, don't get me wrong, and of course lots of money, but his education was rather limited, although he really tries. But it's a bit late now.'

Mel Carlisle stirred his coffee. 'Just say he did walk in now, against all expectations—assuming he didn't do anything dramatic to me, or even if he did, what do you think he'd do to you?'

Rachel considered. 'Nothing I couldn't talk him out of,' she said finally.

'I'm relieved to hear you say so. But I think you might be deluding yourself. Men—have been known to react strangely to these situations.'

Rachel grinned. 'You're the one who keeps coming to see me, Mel. But don't worry, I can handle Joe.'

'Then you must be very confident of your—desirability,' he said, and his grey eyes were completely sober.

Rachel finished her apple and wondered what a woman who was would say to that. But was it such a mystery to any woman? she reflected. 'It's quite simple, really. To be the object of a man's desire is just that—you only have to be anything he wants you to be.'

Their gazes clashed and she felt a faint heat come to her skin as she imagined the kind of visions her words might conjure up for him and suddenly wanted to say... including being a conventional wife who wouldn't want to be travelling around the world with a faintly missionary zeal... Well, not so faint perhaps, she conceded, or you wouldn't be wanting this doctorate so that people might actually listen to you...

'That's it?'

She came out of her reverie just in time to see the contempt in his eyes. She stood up and said lightly, 'It's a pity I'm spoken for, Dr Carlisle. I could give you a crash course otherwise.'

'I find your morals confusing,' he said drily.

'I bet you do, but that's also quite simple,' she retorted. 'Believe it or not, one man at a time is my motto. Things have a habit of getting out of hand otherwise. Will you——?'

But he stood up himself and, before she could move out of reach, he put his hands on her shoulders, turned her to face him.

'In the light of your having Joe in such perfect control, do you mean *I* could get out of hand, Rachel?' he said softly.

'No.' She said it stonily and tried to stare coolly up at him. But it wasn't easy to remain cool as those grey eyes roamed her face and body in a way that was insolently intimate, nor was it easy to be unaware of the feel of his hands through the fine linen shirt, or, to her horror, to be unmoved by his proximity and the tall, beautifully proportioned lines of his body. In fact, it generated in her the first stirrings of desire she'd felt for a long time, and a curiosity about how the act of love would be with this man. As things stood now, an act of conquest, surely, she reasoned, and hated herself for even considering it. 'Let me go,' she said tautly.

But he moved his hands on her shoulders and his thumbs stroked the line of her throat, tilting her chin up, and he kissed her briefly on the lips. Then he dropped his hands and stood back. 'We'll see, Rachel. We'll see.'

She closed her eyes in genuine irritation and something else she couldn't quite define. 'Will you go home—and set your own house to rights? It sounds as if it needs it.'

'It sure does.' He grinned crookedly. 'You wouldn't like to give me a hand?'

'I would not. I've got work to do—just go away and leave me alone.'

'I wonder why I've succeeded in putting you in a temper,' he mused. 'Well, fare thee well, Rachel Wright. I'm going. For the time being. Don't do anything I wouldn't do, such as throwing things,' he said softly, observing her stormy eyes. 'There's already one Meissen figurine to be accounted for, remember.' He went.

Rachel worked on her thesis for the next week with a kind of suppressed fury that left her with a headache and sore eyes at night. The only time she went out was to buy food and to walk for exercise. She'd put the Mercedes back in the garage for storage and discovered that she could satisfy most of her simple needs at the local shops. Besides, she enjoyed walking and each day she ranged a little further from home.

Which was how she managed to get caught in a thunderstorm, two miles from home and laden down with fruit and vegetables, and how Mel Carlisle spotted her and stopped his convertible Saab and offered her a lift home.

'Don't be ridiculous,' he said shortly as she hesitated. 'You look like a drowned rat already!'

'Then I'll soak your car,' she objected.

'The longer you stand there arguing, the more you'll soak it. Get in, Rachel.'

A loud clap of thunder decided the matter. She got in awkwardly, with all her bags trying to impede her, and started to say thank you. But he put the car in gear and shot off, nearly jolting the breath out of her.

She glanced at him and decided that Dr Carlisle was not in a good mood and that, in a conservative charcoal suit, white shirt and discreet maroon tie he looked austere and much more like a distinguished orthopaedic surgeon than he had on the last two occasions they'd met.

'Why are you walking and not driving?' he queried as he changed lanes in the heavy late-afternoon traffic with an arrogance that caused her to lift a wry eyebrow. 'Didn't you appreciate having the Mercedes passed down to you from your predecessor?'

Rachel opened her mouth to deny it but said instead, 'Oh, I'll use it when I need it, but I like to walk. It keeps me in shape.'

'Particularly when there's a lack of bedroom gymnastics to keep you in shape?' he suggested with irony.

Rachel stared down at her hands for a moment. Then she said with a faint smile, 'I'm waiting to see how really insulting you can be Mel. I have the feeling this is a good day for it. What a pity we're so close to home—it's going to curtail your creative genius.'

He said nothing, then deliberately changed lanes again, causing her to clutch the door anxiously then say, 'How you expect to turn right into our street from this lane is something of a mystery to me, Mel.'

'I'm not turning right, Rachel. I agree with you, it would be a pity to curtail my creative genius so early in the piece.' He turned his head briefly and smiled at her but it wasn't a pleasant one. 'I'm taking you out to dinner.'

Rachel took a breath, then cautioned herself to take care how she handled this situation. 'That's very kind of you,' she said evenly, 'but I'm not dressed for dinner and I'm soaking wet— I could catch pneumonia, Dr Carlisle,' she added gently.

'Well, there's an alternative,' he said blandly, and astonished her and not a few Sydney motorists by doing a U-turn where one didn't seem possible. 'You can have dinner with me at my home, after you've dried off. That's my last offer.'

Rachel gritted her teeth. 'And if I don't accept?' she said tautly. 'What will you do then? Continue to drive me round in your car like a spoilt, show-off schoolboy?'

'No,' he said blandly. 'I'll park outside your house—Joe's house, forgive me, Joe—and hoot while the rain lasts, then bang on your door until you come out. Just think how that would enhance the reputation of the neighbourhood.'

'Not to mention your own,' Rachel said through her teeth.

'I couldn't give a damn about my reputation tonight—anyway, Rachel, I've decided, as a newcomer to the street and quite conceivably *unaware* of *your* reputation, I could get away with being considered smitten by my glamorous neighbour and viewed as a poor ignorant fool for a while. Don't you agree?'

'Never for it to be known you're in fact a——'

'Two-faced bastard? Well, no, but then I don't agree with that description, so——'

'You wouldn't,' she said with withering scorn.

He grinned but said softly, 'I'd do it, Rachel. What's it to be?'

She clenched her hands then said coldly. 'I'll come, but over the wall.'

'Ah. Good thinking! There's a ladder on my side but it's not terribly stable—I know, we should devise a code! Why don't you give me two rings on my phone; that'll say, coming over, and three rings would say *you* come over.'

'You...I...' But he drew up outside their houses before she could formulate her furious disgust and she opened the door and gathered her bags.

'Half an hour, Rachel. Would that be long enough to change?' he queried.

She got out and slammed the door. 'Yes!'

The fact that the situation was staggeringly ironic didn't escape her as she showered and changed. That she should have allowed this man to go on thinking what he did of her was of course the most ironic, but there were amusing smaller ironies, she found. Such as her decision to go over the wall, which had been made, she realised, in order to protect his reputation. From the old biddy across the road who also really believed she was...

She stared at herself in Sam's silver-edged bedroom mirror and wondered for a moment if she was entirely sane or if months of living among primitive tribes and in countries where anything could and often did happen had unbalanced her somewhat. Then she decided that it was Mel Carlisle's sheer arrogance and effrontery that had unbalanced her if anything—and, if she was honest, his sheer dangerous attraction. But, she mused, having trodden that path before—although never with a man quite like this—could she afford to do it again? Was that why she was even giving this incredible charade breathing-space—using it as a protection in other words?

It was at this point in her reflections that his features loomed up behind her in the mirror and she frowned, then swung round furiously. 'Don't you ever creep up on me like that again, Dr Carlisle!'

CHAPTER THREE

'MY APOLOGIES, Miss Wright,' Mel said gravely. 'But you're a bit overdue. I was worried about you breaking your neck on the ladder, and I did knock downstairs.' He'd removed his jacket and loosened his tie, and he allowed his grey gaze to roam with approval over her shining dark hair in its ordered cap, the discreet make-up she'd applied, and the beautifully cut jeans she wore with a thin, round-necked buttercup knitted shirt.

Then he turned his attention to the room. 'So——' he looked around with raised eyebrows '—this is where all the action takes place?'

'No, it's not,' she flashed. 'I'm a great believer in variety, so the *salon* floor, the dining-room table—oh, I can be very inventive and unconventional when it comes to that, Mel!'

'You're also quite stunning when you're angry, Rachel—holy hell!' he murmured, wandering into the bathroom, which was dominated by the spa bath the size of a small swimming-pool and set up three steps. 'There too?'

'Get out,' Rachel ordered, but he simply walked over to the bank of built-in wardrobes that lined one wall and pulled the doors open to reveal rail upon rail of clothes.

'I hope these are all yours—I mean, that you didn't inherit them from your predecessor.'

Rachel turned abruptly and walked out. He caught up with her halfway down the stairs. 'Have I seriously offended you?' he queried.

Rachel swore.

He took her hand and prevented her from going any further. 'Why so sensitive suddenly?'

'Sensitive? Suddenly?' she retorted, then wondered why she was—because she'd allowed him to goad her into continuing the charade yet again or because for one breathless moment, she'd imagined sharing the spa bath with him? She tightened her mouth and tried to break free, but uselessly, as his long fingers closed round her wrist and he sat down on a step and pulled her down beside him.

'Calm down, Rachel,' he murmured.

'Calm down!' she marvelled. 'You would trample the sensibilities of a block of wood!'

'I'm not noted for my tact,' he agreed.

'I'm surprised you've even heard of the word!'

'Oh, often. My mother accuses me of a lack of tact frequently.'

'It's a pity you don't take more notice of your mother, then,' she said sardonically.

He turned her hand over thoughtfully. 'That bedroom really embarrasses you, doesn't it?'

'Not for the reasons you imagine,' she retorted, then bit her lip.

'Why, then?'

She hesitated, then said shortly, 'Nothing to do with you.'

'You could tell me, you know. I doubt if I'd be shocked—I might even have seen a bit more of life than you have. I think I'm probably a few years older,' he said.

'If you're thirty-five, as they say, about seven.'

'Well, then—who said I was thirty-five, by the way?'

Rachel sighed and regrouped as best she could. 'Someone at the ball happened to mention it, that's all. What on earth it has to do with us or life in general escapes me,' she said wearily.

'It means I'm not as shockable as I was when I was your age, as I was saying,' he reminded her. 'You didn't by any chance *ask* someone about me at the ball, Rachel?'

She opened her mouth to deny it but realised it was useless as she blushed, something she rarely did, and he saw it and laughed softly. 'So I was right about that, too,' he murmured. 'But I won't press you about the bedroom. You'll probably tell me in your own good time——'

'What is this?' Rachel said irately, because she was still, obviously, off balance. 'Some new and devious plan to rehabilitate me? I thought you were a bone doctor.'

'I am.'

'Well, stick to it,' she advised him. 'I don't need or want anything else.'

'Could you use a drink and a meal?' he asked, his eyes a bland, innocent grey.

She breathed exasperatedly. 'What's suddenly put you in such a good mood?' she demanded. 'I got the distinct impression you were in a foul one when you were showing off in your turbo-charged car.'

'I was. The prospect of dining with you changed all that. Shall we go?'

She made a disgusted sound, and they went.

His house, which he insisted on showing her over from top to bottom, was beautiful. There were pale eggshell colours on the walls and a simplicity everywhere that normally would have been a balm to Rachel's soul. But her soul was in no mood to be soothed, she discovered, and she said little, although she couldn't quite prevent herself from touching the surfaces of some of the exquisitely austere antique pieces of furniture. His bedroom couldn't have been more unlike Sam's. A double bed beneath a plain cream linen spread, a burgundy carpet and matching lampshades on the bedside tables and a tall mahogany chest of drawers with a matching narrow table under the window that was piled with books—mostly medical. One comfortable armchair completed the furniture—but if he expected a comment he got none. Yet she knew he was laughing at her as took her downstairs and into his kitchen, which had a similar breakfast-nook to hers and a similar comforting colonial style.

'Mind if we eat in here?'

'Not at all.'

'What would you like to drink?'

'Scotch and water, please.' She sat down at the table and sniffed rather appreciatively. 'Is cooking another of your talents, Dr Carlisle?'

'No.' He handed her her drink and poured the same thing for himself. 'Well, only the most basic things.'

'Whatever is cooking doesn't smell that basic,' she commented.

'I have this gem of cleaning lady. Whenever she comes in she leaves a casserole for me to heat up. Today she excelled herself and left two. I'm not sure what the second one is, some sort of vegetable concoction.' He sipped his drink then put it down. 'And I have fresh bread, butter—no, don't move, I'll set the table around you. Do you cook, Rachel?'

'I'd starve if I didn't,' she murmured.

'Let me rephrase—do you like to cook?' He pulled a couple of checked napkins from a drawer and added them to the knives and forks and place mats he'd set out around her. Then he got down two crystal wine glasses, took a bottle of Riesling from the refrigerator and stood it in a pottery wine-cooler.

'Yes, I quite enjoy it. I can also sew if I have to and I'm generally fairly domesticated when I need to be.'

'Any good with children?'

'Quite good with other people's children, which doesn't mean much.'

'No burning desire to have some of your own?'

'Obviously not,' she said drily. 'Why the inquisition?'

He shrugged. 'A change of subject, that's all. What would *you* like to talk about?' He was leaning back against a counter with his drink in his hands.

'Tell me about—your mother,' she said after some thought.

He grinned. 'My mother is a very formidable, arrogant lady and I have the misfortune to be her only son as well as her youngest child. I have six sisters, all married with children, all pillars of society but with one great disadvantage from my mother's point of view—they no longer bear the family name.'

Rachel smiled faintly. 'So she's dying for you to get married and provide heirs for the family name—why don't you?'

'I will some day, no doubt.'

'Just waiting for the right girl?' Rachel asked quizzically. 'She'd probably die if she knew you were entertaining me to dinner. She probably has strong views on mistresses.'

'I'm sure she does—most wives do.'

Rachel let that one pass. 'Did she spoil you rotten?'

'She's not really the spoiling kind of mother. In fact, after my father died she was so determined to be the opposite that she was quite painful. We,' he paused, 'have been falling out with great regularity ever since I left home permanently in a rage when I was eighteen. This is an "out" period at the moment.'

'You could be two of a kind,' Rachel mused.

'Oh?' He raised an eyebrow to her.

She laughed. 'Well, you must get your arrogance from somewhere.'

He looked faintly rueful, but not for long. 'You have moments of arrogance yourself, Rachel. Can *you* trace it back to *your* mother?'

'No,' Rachel said, picturing her gentle, often bewildered mother, who would have been the last person one would have expected to have the fortitude to bear a child in flea-ridden tent in Morocco. 'If it's there, it must come from my father's side.'

'How do you think your mother and father—do they know what you do for a living?' he queried.

'No. Well, they're both dead—I thought we were changing the subject?'

He was about to say something but a bell pinged and he said instead, 'Dinner's ready. How fortuitous.'

Dinner was delicious, a chicken casserole; the vegetable concoction proved to be courgette, tomato and onion beneath a cheese topping. When he got a phone call of an obviously medical nature just after they'd eaten it, Rachel cleared up quietly.

That showed her another side of Mel Carlisle because when he put the phone down after about twenty minutes he turned round and, for a bare moment, looked at her as if she was a complete stranger. Then he looked round and said, 'You didn't have to do that.'

She shrugged and picked up her wine glass. 'I'll finish this and go. It sounds to me as if you have a delicate, marathon operation on tomorrow. Is that——' she wasn't sure why it occurred to her but it did '—why you were in such an impossible mood earlier?'

He sat down and said briefly, 'Partly.'

'Are you afraid it won't be successful?' she asked quietly and noted that he'd only had one glass of wine, so she rose and started to make coffee.

'It'll be successful if it's the last thing I do.' He sat back and shoved his hands in his pocket. 'But he's only a kid and I've operated on the poor, brave little beggar more times than I care to remember. I keep telling myself it's hurting him more than me, but...'

Rachel said nothing and went on making the coffee. But when she handed him his cup she said thoughtfully, 'You should devise a formula to help you deal with your tension. Other than frightening the lives out of respectable Sydney motorists.'

'Oh, I have.'

Her eyes narrowed at the way his rested on her with a glint that was part mockery, part something else. 'I see,' she said at last and with contempt.

'What do you see, Rachel?' he asked softly. 'I thought you more than most would understand the tension-reducing values of sex.'

'That depends,' she said steadily and was surprised at her steadiness. 'How do you do it? Do you have a roster system or do just go out and find someone for the night?'

'Are either of those things any worse than— being what any man with enough money wants you to be, dear Rachel?'

'I've said this before,' she stood up, 'but I'll say it again: you run your life, Mel, and leave me to run mine.' She turned towards the back door but he was up in one quick, lithe movement and barring her way.

'Going back to that silver and blue *prison*, Rachel?'

'I'm certainly not staying here to be insulted and slept with on a tension-reducing basis, if that's what you had in mind. Get out your little black book, Doctor, and get out of my way!' she commanded.

'All right,' he murmured, and slid his hands about her waist. 'When I've done this.'

He was both amazingly strong when it came to resisting her furious struggle for freedom, and amazingly competent when it came to kissing her once her strength ran out, and he did a lot of it with his hands, she realised, breathing erratically and suddenly feeling her skin come alive beneath those wandering fingers even through her knitted top. Another thought that came to plague her was that it had been so long since she'd been caressed and held by a man. In fact, never by one as expert as this, who knew exactly where to tantalise her then quieten her, and start again until she was trembling in his arms not only from the responses of her own body but also from the primitive, sheer male onslaught of his. So that when his mouth finally sought hers she was helpless with a longing to blend even closer.

But, while it was a kiss that started out as a submission, it soon lit a fire of desire in her so that she was kissing back with a kind of fierceness and hunger that dimly amazed her.

And, when it ended, she fell back in his arms, gasping for breath and more truly aroused than she'd ever been. 'Oh, God,' she said hoarsely. 'What do think you're doing?'

He studied her bruised mouth and flushed cheeks through half-closed lids, and moved his hands across the small of her back. 'You owed me that, Rachel.'

'I owe you nothing!' she breathed.

'Yes, you do. Do you really want to know why I was in such a foul mood this afternoon? I'll tell you. It suddenly dawned on me when I saw you standing in the rain, still looking so proud and beautiful, that there's only one person I want to go to bed with at the moment—and that is you. Don't you feel you ought to take some responsibility for that?' His eyes mocked her.

'No. I——'

'And then the other thing that motivated me just now was the desire to see if I *could* set someone as basically cold and mercenary as you alight. Really alight, I mean, as opposed to acting out some man's fantasy. I think I succeeded, don't you?'

'I think you're mad,' she whispered.

'Nevertheless, you certainly came alight, Rachel.'

She took a quick, despairing breath. 'You ...'

'I ...?' He waited.

'Oh—let me go!'

He released her promptly. 'Lost for words?' he said softly. 'Why don't you for once in your life do something *honest*, Rachel? Why don't you run out on Joe and move in with me? At least,' he said, 'you could go to bed with me as yourself. And because you actually want it.'

'You're——' Rachel's voice cracked '—asking me to be your mistress?'

'Well, in view of your ability to be beautiful and tantalising and to play at studying agricultural economics,' he said with open contempt, 'but with no visible means of support, it couldn't be any other way, could it?'

If she'd been flushed and dishevelled before, she was now white and her blue eyes glittered like sapphires. 'And just how long do you think that would last?' she asked, possessed, she realised, of an anger deeper than she could remember. 'You despise me already—no, thank you, Mel, there just isn't enough future in it for me. Think how relieved your mother will be!' she taunted. 'As for *honesty*——'

'I'm not asking you to be unfaithful to Joe,' he drawled. 'Just to admit you'd rather sleep with me than him—isn't that your motto: one man at a time? Which is your brand of faithfulness, I presume. And I guess no man could ask for more unless he's got his wedding-ring on your finger. And if you don't possess a stitch of anything he hasn't provided you with, come stitchless. I would of course be prepared to clothe you. Although we wouldn't need to rush into it,' he said with a smile lurking in his eyes.

'How...kind of you. I still must decline,' Rachel stammered. 'And on the subject of darkening doorsteps, may I take this opportunity to warn you that if you ever darken mine again, I will call the police? Let me through.'

He didn't move. 'I think I get it,' he said slowly. 'Even mistresses expect to be courted—perhaps more so than wives! In fact they're probably very sensitive about it; after all, it is a step up the ladder from just selling one's body indiscriminately, isn't it? I mean, there's your intellectualism to be taken into account, and your sense of style, not to mention your inventiveness—of course all that must call for skilful, delicate negotiation. Why didn't I think of it?' he marvelled. But he went on in a different, suddenly ruthless way. 'Unless it just comes down to dollars and cents. I don't know how many of them Joe has, but in case you don't know it——'

'Stop. Stop it,' Rachel said huskily, and paused herself to choose her words with care. 'Your summing up of me may be perfectly accurate from what you feel you know about me. It's...in fact it's accurate from what you don't know, which is really rather ironic, but it boils down to this—I don't want to have anything more to do with you, Mel. You've not the kind of man I could live with, for several reasons. I won't bother you with the bulk of them, but this one I will. You're the kind of hypocrite I could never live with.'

'And Joe's no hypocrite?' he said with a dangerous glitter in his eyes.

'Leave Joe out of it. *You're* the one who thinks he can buy a woman he basically despises...' She stopped as his eyes narrowed alertly suddenly, and she wondered if she'd given herself away, but immediately asked herself what difference it would make. He was still the man who had mistaken her so completely, and the same man who could arouse her, yet be like this and express a fundamental cynicism that had to be part of him, whatever he knew or didn't—the last man she should allow herself to love. Then some inner demon, of hurt perhaps, prompted her to add, 'Even whores have their pride, you know. Goodnight.'

He let her go this time.

It was unfortunate that brief, ridiculous tears blurred her vision just long enough to make her miss her footing and crash off the marble table on her side of the wall.

She cried out, then lay winded and biting her lip, but he'd heard and he was over the wall himself, cursing roughly then swinging her up in his arms. 'I'm all right,' she said weakly.

'Like hell you are—where's your key?'

'Mel——' But he put her down outside the french door and one ankle gave way, causing him to swear again and gather her keys out of her jeans pocket while she rocked on one foot and had to clutch at him as he opened the door. Then he picked her up again and marched in with her and straight up the stairs.

'Look——'

'Shut up, Rachel,' he commanded, and set her down on the bed.

'But I don't think it's serious,' she protested.

He took no notice and bent over her left ankle, probing it gently as she winced with pain. 'Take your jeans off.'

'No! Mel——'

'Listen, if you don't take them off now, I'm going to have to cut them off. It's starting to swell.'

'But——'

'Rachel, I am a doctor,' he said sardonically. 'Just do it.'

Rachel moved agitatedly, gasped with pain and glanced down at her ankle, which indeed was swelling rapidly. 'Oh, all right,' she muttered, encountering his grey gaze again, and with his help managed to slide out of her jeans. Then he sat down, picked up her foot and moved it about, watching her reactions narrowly. Finally he put it down. 'I don't think it's broken, but we'll need X-rays. And in the meantime ice.'

Incredibly, in a short space of time she was sitting propped up on her bed with her foot propped on another pillow complete with ice-bag. And Mel was on the phone.

She watched him as he roamed impatiently around the room with the phone. He'd discarded his tie and rolled up his shirt-sleeves and he looked the picture of what he essentially was: a dark, arrogant, dangerously attractive man.

His call went along the lines of, 'Marty, it's Mel. Listen, my neighbour has hurt her ankle. Can you bring your portable machine round? Marty, you owe me one, old son, and if it's that little first-year nurse you should be ashamed of yourself.' He listened for a moment, then grinned his crooked grin. 'Will do. Uh—on your way, chat up Sister Surgical and get a pair of crutches and a bandage from her—tell her it's for me.' He put receiver and phone together and brought them back to the bedside table. 'He won't be long. He's an old friend of mine.'

'Is this going to cost me an arm and a leg?' Rachel enquired.

'It's all free; comes with the—neighbourhood.'
'I see.'

He gazed down at her. 'You wouldn't have anything like an ordinary, respectable pair of pyjamas, would you? Marty's a bit impressionable.'

'Yes, I do,' Rachel said coolly, and rummaged under the pillow, 'but I can manage perfectly well, Doctor, in case you had ideas of helping me.'

'Never entered my head,' he drawled. 'I do have a reputation to protect, you know. I'll go down and wait for Marty.' He closed the door behind him.

Rachel glared at it, then painfully changed into the least revealing of Sam's nightwear she'd been able to find, a very tailored pair of white silk pyjamas with blue dots and piping.

She was just lying back feeling exhausted when there was a knock on the door.

Marty was a very friendly, slightly overweight, shaggy man with freckles and laughing blue eyes. Whether the laughter had been prompted by Sam's opulent décor or he always looked like that, Rachel couldn't tell, but he did manage to be the soul of propriety and admiring gallantry at the same time—no mean feat. He also didn't let his friend Mel off the hook.

'How come my neighbours always resemble dogs?' he grumbled cheerfully as he set up his machine. 'You know, Miss Wright, Melville here has the most astounding luck.'

'Melville?' Rachel said with an involuntary quirk of her lips.

Mel cast his mate a sardonic look. 'Thanks.'

'It gets worse. Melville Fitzroy Carlisle—his mother——'

'I've told Miss Wright about my mother, Marty,' Mel said wearily.

'So you two know each other quite well!' Marty said ingenuously. 'You'd have to. Mel normally keeps her a dead secret. I remember the day she——'

'Oh for God's sake, Marty,' Mel growled. 'Just get on with the job—anyone would think we were still in med. school, the way you carry on.'

'I believe I do have something of the eternal schoolboy in me,' Marty said complacently, and manoeuvred Rachel's ankle gently. 'How did this happen, by the way?'

'She—fell off a table.'

'Ah! Tricky things, tables, for standing or sitting on, I mean.'

'Rachel normally has a way with them,' Mel said coolly, and for an instant their gazes clashed—his loaded with irony, hers saying—you bastard!

Unfortunately, Marty intercepted this clash and his shaggy eyebrows shot up, but he contented himself with a little whistle and proceeded to be very professional while he took his pictures, though he couldn't quite hide the speculation in his eyes every time they rested on Rachel. Then he explained he'd have to take the X-rays away to get developed, which he probably wouldn't be able to do before morning, and insisted on demonstrating and fitting the crutches. 'I think you'd be best off staying here tucked up for the night, anyway,' he finished.

'So do I,' Rachel agreed rather palely.

'Is there anyone who could come and stay with you—I gather you're on your own?'

'No. I'll be fine. Thank you.'

'No problems.' He started packing things up. 'And Mel's right next door anyway,' he added significantly. 'Well,' he straightened up and couldn't quite help himself from looking around rather quizzically this time. 'I'll leave you two to it. Let you know in the morning, old man, but I agree with you, I don't think it's broken; still, better to be sure than sorry——'

'Come on, I'll see you out,' Mel said with palpable irritation.

What took place during this procedure, Rachel could only guess at, but guessed she was right when Mel returned looking in an even worse mood than he had earlier in the day.

'It was all your idea,' she said, fighting an insane desire to laugh.

'Are you saying I should have left you lying there with a possibly broken ankle?' he shot at her.

'No. I'm grateful you didn't.'

'Then what are you looking so amused about?' he grated.

Rachel laid her head back. 'Your friend. The deductions he's made——'

'If you didn't live in a...a place that closely resembles a bordello, he might have accepted it was simply a neighbourly act——'

'Until he saw us exchanging extremely un-neighbourly glances, he might have, although I doubt it. Will it be all over the hospital tomorrow?' she asked with gentle satire.

'What exactly do you think his deductions are?' he asked, more restrainedly but with a dangerous dryness.

Rachel shrugged. 'That the great Mel Carlisle, doctor extraordinaire, has got himself entangled with a woman he—Marty, I mean—didn't know what the hell to make of himself.'

She saw him relax, saw the tension go out of his shoulders and should have been prepared, but wasn't.

'Oh, I think Marty realises exactly what kind of woman you are, my dear. It's written all over you,' he said softly.

Rachel sat up abruptly, then flinched. 'Get out,' she whispered.

'Just going.'

It amazed her that, through all her rather tortured recriminations, castigations and general disgust with the series of events that had befallen her and in particular those of the last evening, she could still wonder how a certain operation on a certain brave child was going.

She got the news via Marty the next morning that her ankle wasn't broken. He called personally; she was downstairs, having had to negotiate the stairs on her bottom.

'Well, that's good news,' she said briefly, balancing on her crutches and preparing to close the door on him.

He had other ideas. 'Listen, I'm dying of curiosity,' he said honestly.

'Then prepare to drop dead,' Rachel retorted unkindly. 'You sure you're not just a simple voyeur posing as a radiologist?'

'I don't think so. I have a certain vested interest, you see. Mel is one of my oldest as well as best friends. We were at school together even before med. school and I've got this feeling that you hate him and that he doesn't know whether he wants to murder you or—the other thing, which would be an entirely new sensation for him, believe me. And not before time!'

Rachel stared at him, then, on an impulse, opened the door wider awkwardly. 'Take another look around,' she said curtly. 'What do you think this is?'

Marty stepped in, gazed at the nude on the wall then said, taking Rachel by surprise. 'I don't make snap judgements. Even if it is what it looks like, I wouldn't condemn you out of hand until I knew you better; there could be all sorts of reasons for it. Is that what Mel did?'

Rachel laughed a little bitterly. 'He hasn't even seen it. But anyway, it's none of your business, and when you talk about knowing me better, don't——'

'Rachel—may I call you that?' Marty said, and she was surprised again to see that he was looking at her quite soberly. 'Rachel, I think someone should explain Mel to you. I often feel in fact that *someone* should put out an explanatory video on him, it would save a lot of broken hearts. May I?'

'Well——'

Ten minutes later they were seated in the breakfast nook drinking tea.

'He's always been too darn brilliant for his own good,' Marty began, tucking into a shortbread biscuit. 'Brilliant at school, a brilliant cricketer when he was interested, he can play the piano like an angel—and of course, the apple of his mother's eye. A son, after six daughters, generally is.'

'From what he's told me, his mother is a tyrant.'

'She likes to think she is, but she met her match in Mel—I guess we all did,' he said affectionately. 'Then there was all that lovely money he inherited when his father died——'

'Hang on,' Rachel said slowly, and couldn't believe this hadn't occurred to her before. 'He's not one of *those* Carlisles?'

'None other. Shipping, brewing—he was in fact the sole heir; well, Mum and sisters were provided for very, very handsomely of course, but the bulk is his. Nor does it stop there. His mother is a prominent member of the landed gentry; she was a Fitzroy—I think she might have been able to bear the fact that Mel wasn't into shipping and brewing, but the fact that's he's not into the *land* is more than any blue-blooded squatter's daughter can bear.'

'I see,' Rachel said slowly.

'Mmm,' Marty agreed. 'Now, whatever a tyrant your mum is, it's impossible not be spoiled and have everything you could ever desire in those circumstances. It also does him great credit that he persisted in doing the one thing he wanted to in the face of universal opposition.'

'Why shouldn't they have wanted him to be a doctor?'

'Possibly because looking after the Carlisle interests is more than enough for one man to do—naturally they expected him to have some kind of university background, but one that would either lend itself specifically to running the show, or would have fitted him out to be a gentleman of taste and discrimination.'

'So he fought his mother and won,' Rachel said, and might as well have said, big deal!

Marty grinned. 'Oh, I think you're going to be so good for him, Rachel. You see, his other problem is that women have been flinging themselves at his feet since—well,' he gestured, 'primary-school days.'

Rachel sipped her tea thoughtfully. 'None of this——' she said eventually, and paused. 'Well, it might explain some things, but it doesn't change the fact that he's an arrogant——'

'Son of a bitch?'

'You said it. And probably will never change.'

Marty pursed his lips. 'He does have another side. This kid he's operating on this morning—he comes from a penniless Filipino family. Mel's footing the bill and donating his services. And he's only one of many. Mel's set up a trust out of the family fortune—and, believe me, Rachel, he's not only a genius with a scalpel, he's a dedicated doctor.'

'A regular Dr Jekyll and Mr Hyde,' Rachel murmured.

Marty whistled. 'He has set your back up.'

Rachel sighed suddenly. 'Owing to an unbelievable set of circumstances, I've contributed my share, Marty, but it would never have worked anyway. Would you do me a favour? Just forget you ever met me.'

'I doubt if I could, but I won't be gossiping, if that's what you mean.'

Rachel coloured faintly and offered him some more shortbread.

CHAPTER FOUR

SHE was sitting in the kitchen that evening, eating a dinner composed of baked beans on toast, when he came over the wall and let himself in without knocking.

'What do you want now?' Rachel said wearily after a moment, warily and tersely because she'd been unprepared for the little jolt of her heartbeat when she saw how tired he looked. She had in fact spent periods on and off throughout the day reasoning out just why it would be the utmost folly on her part to fall in love with Mel Carlisle, and had comforted herself with the knowledge that she was only human and that that was why she'd responded physically to him the way she had.

'Any left?' he asked, and wandered over to the pot on the stove. There were, and he didn't bother to put them on a plate, he just got a spoon and brought the pot over to the table.

'Isn't it your cleaning lady's day? You can't exist on half a can of baked beans,' she said acidly.

'You are,' he murmured.

'I haven't been working all day. How—did it go?' She just couldn't help herself, she found.

'Cautiously optimistic. I'll know more in a couple of weeks. How's the ankle?'

'Better. It's not broken.'

'I know. Marty rang me. You're right.' He stood up again. 'I'm starving.'

Rachel watched as he raided the refrigerator and came back with a wedge of cheese and a bottle of pickles. He then collected the bread and butter and proceeded to make himself several enormous cheese and pickle sandwiches, and a pot of tea. 'Want some?'

'Just the tea, thanks. Has it occurred to you that you have an incredible nerve, Mel?' she asked conversationally, somewhat to her surprise.

He grinned and poured her tea. 'Do you mean after the insults I offered you yesterday?'

'Something like that—your last one, anyway.'

'That rankled, did it? I apologise, that wasn't quite true.'

'You astonish me,' she said softly.

'Well, I guess if you didn't astonish *me*, Rachel, we wouldn't be doing this,' he replied.

'We're only *doing* this because I have little option to do otherwise at the moment,' she pointed out coldly.

'You could have locked the door.'

'Why should I live like a——?'

'Prisoner? I don't know, you tell me,' he invited.

Rachel subsided into a frustrated silence which he took advantage of to demolish his sandwiches. He then drank his tea thirstily and poured himself another cup.

'I've come to make a proposition,' he said finally.

'Oh, no——'

'Just listen, Rachel.' A glint of his old impatience lit his eyes. 'I'm taking a few days off this weekend, Friday to Monday. Come with me—my intentions are entirely honourable, I won't lay a finger on you unless you invite me to, it's a house party as a matter of fact and they'll all be very proper people.' He smiled slightly. 'Your ankle should be much better by then.'

Rachel stared at him with her lips parted. Then she said huskily, clutching at straws, she realised, 'Joe...' And trailed off, despising herself.

'Look, you're not *married* to the man. And it'll be entirely up to you how you handle your side of the matter. For that matter, entirely up to you whether you come or not. I'm not proposing to kidnap you.'

'But what you *are* proposing is stealing me——'

'Stealing you be damned,' he said irritably. 'What the hell are you, Rachel? You tell me you're your own woman, you tell me you have your own principles, that no man can dictate to you—I presumed you were telling me you weren't just a good old-fashioned concubine with little say in the matter, but now I have to wonder. Or is it something else altogether? Are you basically a frightened woman? Frightened, for some reason, of a real, no-holds-barred involvement with a man?'

It was only much later that she realised that what she did then was a denial, to herself as much as to him, that she was frightened of him and afraid of falling in love with him and facing the same old story—not, she doubted, that Mel Carlisle would want to marry her.

She said slowly, 'What do you think these proper people would think if they knew...what I am?'

'They won't know,' he said simply.

'And if after these few days I'm still of the same mind as I am now, will you leave me in peace?'

'Yes.'

'Then I'll come.' She looked at him defiantly.

'That's a change of heart,' he said softly, and that oddly alert look was back in his eyes.

'So is yours,' she countered, clamping down on her anger. 'Last night you were offering to do much more than lay a finger on me. I wonder if I can trust you an inch, Mel?'

'Talking of last night, how far do you think you can trust yourself?'

Rachel narrowed her eyes. 'Just don't pull the old trick of having us arrive and find we have to share a bedroom,' she warned.

He laughed. 'That would be a test, wouldn't it?'

'I'd walk straight out again, Mel.'

'All right!' He stretched and got up and walked around restlessly, picking things up and putting them down.

'What is it now?' Rachel enquired finally.

'I don't feel like going to bed yet.'

'You should. How long did you operate for?'

He shrugged. 'Seven hours.'

Rachel watched his back as he stared moodily out over the darkened courtyard, then she said,

'From what Marty told me about you today, you would only have to lift the phone to have some . . . one come and help you——' she paused significantly '—unwind.'

'Ah, but, as I mentioned yesterday, I don't want just—anyone now. So Marty's been spilling state secrets.' He turned back and his eyes were amused.

Rachel put her head on one side consideringly. 'Marty feels you're a . . . walking disaster where women are concerned. He feels you need help, or at least the girls you get involved with do, and he set himself up in an advisory capacity to me this morning.'

Mel Carlisle uttered a sentiment that was highly uncomplimentary towards his absent friend. 'What else did he tell you?'

'Well I got the impression that you were once a poor little—very rich boy, and I've got the feeling you've never quite outgrown it,' Rachel said meditatively.

There was a sudden dangerously silent moment as their eyes clashed. 'Don't for one minute imagine you're dealing with a boy, Rachel,' he said softly at last, and his eyes roamed over her in a way that left her in no doubt that he was in fact a very experienced man—something she'd never doubted anyway.

She lowered her lashes as her skin began to prickle almost as if his fingers were on it, but she soldiered on. 'In some respects, obviously not,' she murmured. 'But you just might have carried over a dangerous inability to cope with being thwarted in any way.'

'As a matter of fact, you could be right, Rachel,' he said barely audibly. 'So just remember it the next time you decide to look beautiful and untouchable and decide to lecture me on all my shortcomings at the same time.'

'Is that a threat?' she said steadily, her eyes deepening to an angry blue.

His stared at her then his lips twisted wryly, 'In fact it's a rather gentlemanly instinct—you're at a physical disadvantage at the moment, so you're quite safe. Now.'

Rachel raised her eyes heavenwards. 'If that isn't twisting things round to suit your own devious purposes—look, why don't you just go home? You've achieved what you set out to achieve—— '

'I've got a better idea—there is something else that relaxes me. Let's listen to some music together. I promise to behave with the utmost propriety. Are you in the mood for Bach tonight? Or what about Mozart? You choose. Don't bother with your crutches.'

'You're impossible,' she said as he carried her into the *salon*.

'I know.'

'*And* all the other things I've ever said about you.'

He stopped with her in his arms in the middle of the *salon* and looked down at her quite soberly. 'Perhaps. But I want you, Rachel, more than I've wanted anything for a while.'

Her mouth trembled and she thought of saying, Yes, but what happens when you stop wanting me, when you find out what I really am—even

if you don't...? And to her amazement she
turned her face into his shirt for a moment, to
hide her eyes.

They stood like that for a long moment before
she sniffed and looked up at the strange look in
his eyes. 'You'd better put me down,' she said
huskily. 'And yes, make it Mozart but no
Requiem or *Don Giovanni*. No,' she added as he
made to speak, 'nothing's changed, but I need a
break.'

He gave her a break.

They listened to music and chatted about anything but themselves. He made coffee later and
poured liqueurs, and he made himself quite at
home on the yellow settee, taking his shoes off
and putting his long legs up, and then falling
asleep.

Rachel, when she realised it, watched him for
what seemed a long time. He even managed to
sleep with a sort of sprawled, careless grace, and
his face, in repose, was younger. Then she laid
her head back and closed her eyes, and tried to
picture the kind of woman he would eventually
marry—and decided that what he would need was
a woman like her mother, able to devote herself
exclusively, capable of an enduring passion
almost to the exclusion of all else, even a child.

It was his pager, clipped to his belt, that jolted
her out of her bleak reverie and jolted him awake.

He sat up, rubbed his face wearily and ran his
hands through his hair, and her heart went out
to him. He'd slept for little more than half an

hour. And once again, as his eyes rested on her, she might have been a complete stranger.

Then he blinked and grimaced. 'Sorry—why didn't you wake me?'

'I thought you deserved a rest. I would have, eventually. Is that,' she nodded at his beeper, 'a call from the hospital?'

'Yes. I'll have to dash. Uh, can I help you up to bed, or——'

She shook her head. 'Just get my crutches. And do me a favour: don't come back until Friday.'

It was a beautiful summer morning when he collected her quite openly from her front door, with the roof of his Saab down. 'Ah,' he said picking up her one small case—Sam's Vuitton case to be precise. 'A woman who knows how to travel light is a woman after my own heart. Few do.'

'I've had plenty of practice.'

'Of course. How's your ankle?'

'As you predicted, much better.' She got in. 'How far do we have to go?' she asked as he started the motor.

'It's about a four-hour drive.'

'I hope you're in a good mood,' she murmured.

'Pretty good. Why?'

'You're a terrifying driver when you're not.'

He laughed. 'I'm actually a very safe driver, Rachel. Fear not. I have a flair for it.'

'Your flair for modesty is also remarkable.'

He glanced at her. 'I gather you're filled with doubts about this.'

She gripped her hands in her lap.

'You certainly look the part,' he said lightly.
'*What* part?'

'Don't get your hackles up! The part of an impending house guest, casually elegant. Beautiful as always,' he added quietly.

'I don't always look like this,' Rachel murmured. 'In fact I can look . . . quite unremarkable at times. Um, you'd better tell me more about this house party.'

It was a pleasant drive. They stopped for lunch at a hamlet in the Blue Mountains then continued north-west to the wide open plains around Mudgee. Their hosts owned a horse stud, as Mel had explained, and were long-standing friends of the Carlisle family. As they finally drew up in front of the grand old two-storeyed colonial mansion, miles and miles from anywhere, Rachel deduced that they were also on a par with the Carlisle family, money-wise.

There were several cars parked on the gravel circle in front of the house, one of which caused Mel to narrow his eyes then swear beneath his breath. Before she could ask why, two people and at least six dogs erupted down the front veranda steps, and the opportunity was lost.

'Mel, old son, great to see you! And you must be Rachel. Welcome to Lilianvale! I'm Peter Stevens and this is my wife Sally.'

Peter and Sally Stevens were both in their forties, Rachel judged and, while he was tall and lean, Sally was a diminutive redhead with a warm, bubbling personality. 'We're so glad Mel brought you.' She put her arm through Rachel's.

It was then that Mel said, 'I see you also invited,' he nodded towards the car that had caught his eye earlier, 'the grand duchess herself.'

Sally laughed. 'Well, Mel, darling,' she lowered her voice, 'we didn't. *She* invited herself at the very last minute—and you know how hard it is to refuse her anything. But it is time you two patched things up...er——' Sally Stevens exchanged a glance with her husband '—she did also bring——'

But a very upright, superbly groomed woman appeared at the steps and started to descend, saying in a clear, cultured voice, 'Don't bother to apologise, Sally. I will take the blame. How are you, Mel? It seems a bit ridiculous that I have to descend to these levels to see you, but there you are.'

Rachel's eyes widened, but although the dark hair was streaked with grey there was no mistaking where Mel Carlisle had got his grey eyes and his arrogant air from—his mother.

There was a moment of silence as mother and son stared at each other and the tension in the air was palpable. Then Mel relaxed with a dry smile. 'Beloved, you're right. We really should learn to tolerate each other in a more civilised manner.'

To which his mother replied, equally drily, 'I do hope you're not going to be as ungracious as you can be at times, Mel. We wouldn't want to make everyone uncomfortable, now, would we? By the way, I brought Fiona with me; she was at a loose end this weekend—she's down looking at the horses. Fiona and Mel,' Mrs Carlisle said, turning directly to Rachel, 'have known each other for years and are such good friends. How do you do? I don't believe we've met.'

'No, you haven't, Mother,' Mel said swiftly. 'This is my mother, Rachel. Mother this is Rachel Wright—soon to be Carlisle, however, as soon as I can persuade her to set the date.'

'I don't believe this.' Rachel rubbed her face dazedly. 'How *could* you?'

It was a bare, stunned, strained half-hour since Mel had dropped his bombshell and they were now in the pretty bedroom that opened on to the upstairs veranda alloted to Rachel, where Mel had carried her bag, and was now leaning against the closed door, his shoulders shaking with laughter.

'Stop it!' she said fiercely. 'How dare you——? Oh, of all the insults and sheer——'

'As a matter of fact,' he straightened, his eyes still amused, 'you're the first person I've asked to marry me, and that's not generally regarded as an insult.'

'You didn't *ask* me to marry you!' Rachel raged. 'Which would be the last thing I'd do anyway. You made it all up on the spur of the moment to get back at your mother. Why? Or——' She stopped, her eyes narrowing. 'Has it something to do with this poor Fiona person?'

'You're very quick on the uptake, Rachel,' he murmured appreciatively. 'It has a lot to do with her. My mother has been trying to marry me off for years, as I think I told you once, but her very favourite candidate has always been Fiona—by the way, you don't need to feel sorry for her.

Fiona can more than take care of herself. But I'm tired of the whole damn business,' he said abruptly.

'You—I keep thinking there's nothing more you can do to amaze me, Mel, but you keep surprising me. None of this has *anything* to do with me in the first place——'

'That's debatable, but go on.'

'Listen, let's not pretend I wouldn't be the last person you'd marry,' she flung at him. 'Then there's the fact that you've placed me in an extremely... a totally impossible situation this weekend, and, if you ask me, *Fiona*, whatever she's like, wouldn't *be* here if she didn't have some ambitions towards you, so she's in an impossible position too!'

'Look, I agree that matrimony might not have entered either of our calculations, but we are here to sort out our—inclinations towards each other. We are here, to put it bluntly, to test each other out——'

'No, I'm here to *prove* to you I can resist you and all your money and your offers to make me your *mistress*,' she said scathingly.

'Rachel,' he raised an eyebrow at her, 'it's just crossed my mind to wonder whether your being here isn't part of a much more subtle campaign than my mother would ever have dreamt of—to acquire yourself a wedding-ring.'

She went to hit him in a flash of white-hot rage, but ended up in his arms with her wrists clamped behind her back. 'Temper, temper,' he said softly. 'Did I hit a nerve? You know, one day I'll kiss you when you're soft and compliant, and begging for it.'

She was in helpless tears in fact, when his mouth left hers at last, and it helped not one whit that he held her shaking body close quite gently until she regained some composure, then stood her away from him thoughtfully with his hands on her shoulders.

'Listen, Mel,' she wiped her eyes with the back of her hand, 'enough is enough. I'm not what you think I am. I——'

'Oh, I know there's some deep dark mystery there, but, you see, I'm not entirely what you think I am either.' He slid his fingers down to her wrists. 'Just do this for me, Rachel. Go along with me this weekend. I'm never going to marry just to please my mother, and the sooner she understands that, the less of this kind of nonsense I'll have to put up with.'

There was a knock on the door, then it opened about an inch and a strange voice asked if it was all right to come in.

Mel gritted his teeth then said irritably, 'Yes, Fiona, you might as well!'

Fiona was blonde, tall and stunningly attractive. She was also amazingly forthright—after a moment of summing Rachel up in an extremely comprehensive way, even to the tear-streaks. In fact Rachel got the feeling that Fiona not only knew she was exactly five feet six in bare feet, weighed a hundred and twelve pounds, wore a Stuart Membury outfit of trousers and a cropped, short-sleeved jacket, shoes by Charles Jourdan, make-up by Christian Dior, hair by Mr Leon,

Anne Lewin underwear and perfume by Nina Ricci—but that she was also a fraud.

She said, however, as she draped herself on the bed and crossed her own jodphur-clad legs, 'You've really done it this time, Mel! Your mother is incensed, I suppose I should be...something, but I'm damned if I'm going to be made to look a fool. So you'd better introduce me to your fiancée, and I'll take her down to afternoon tea. Poor Sally and Peter are nervous wrecks!' She chuckled.

Mel stared down at her, his mouth set in a hard line.

'Oh, come on, darling!' Fiona purred. 'Somehow or other we've got to rescue this weekend—there *are* other guests, you know. I promise I won't play the jilted girlfriend or turn vicious on—it's Rachel, isn't it?' She turned to Rachel. 'You've been crying. I wonder why? Providing you haven't *trapped* Mel into marriage and he hasn't got you from behind the perfume counter at David Jones or somewhere worse, like a brothel; providing you're not a first-year nurse or any kind of nurse—Mrs C. has always had a dread of anything as common as a nurse; providing you're not a divorcee or a Muslim or a radical feminist or a career woman—being a Carlisle woman is all the career you'll be allowed; providing you don't eat your peas with your knife and your asparagus with your fork...his mother will get over it.' She switched her bold gaze back to Mel.

'Have you quite finished?' he asked dispassionately.

'I think so. Did I leave something out?'

'Yes,' Rachel said, huskily. 'Thank you for your offer, but I can take care of myself. As a matter of fact I'm several of the things you mentioned, but I'll leave you to guess which ones. One other thing: I haven't accepted Mel's offer yet; he—rather jumped the gun. Perhaps that will bring some comfort to his mother—perhaps you'd like to pass on the news, Fiona? We'll be down shortly.'

Mel said, surprisingly, as the door closed on Fiona, 'That was rather clever. It definitely links us but obviates the need for involved pretences— is that why you did it?'

Rachel sat down on the bed abruptly. 'I did it because I'm not about to be patronised by anyone this weekend, Mel, or manipulated. But believe me, if I could walk off this place I would!'

'You're angry,' he said consideringly. 'What was it? Brothels, or the way you might eat your peas?'

'Of course I'm angry, and no, it was neither of those, it's being in this ridiculous position at all. It's *you*.'

'Look, I've got a suggestion to make.'

Rachel closed her eyes. 'Don't,' she begged. 'I'm only in this mess because of your last suggestion.'

'This might surprise you. Reserve your anger for me if you like, but give everyone downstairs the benefit of the real Rachel Wright.'

Rachel opened her eyes wide. 'What do you mean?'

'Just be yourself.'

'How can I be myself if I'm supposed to be madly in love with you?'

'But you've just sent Fiona away with a flea in her ear—and the impression that *I'm* madly in love with *you*, whereas you are not committed yet nor at all sure if you want to be. That,' he said, 'wouldn't be terribly far from the truth.'

'But you're not madly in love with me, and——'

'I'm,' a wry smile lit his eyes, 'madly attracted to you. And, despite your fighting it every inch of the way, you are—intrigued.'

'Oh!' Rachel stood up with, with an exasperated groan. 'You never give up, do you?'

He didn't answer, just watched her pace around the room enigmatically.

'You've already broken your promise,' she accused him.

He shrugged. 'That was in the nature of self-defence. You might have given me a black eye.' He said it perfectly gravely, but of course there was nothing grave about the wicked little glint in his eye.

Rachel's shoulders sagged suddenly—how did you cope with Mel Carlisle? How did you stay angry with him when all your senses suddenly betrayed you and you remembered the feel of his arms around you, the hard strength of his body— and the way that made you feel in his arms?

He came towards her and stopped right in front of her but didn't attempt to touch her. 'Rachel?' he said at last, after they'd stared into each other's eyes for a long moment.

'All right,' she whispered. 'But I'm not taking any—nonsense from anybody,' she added with more spirit. 'You included.'

'That's my girl. Shall we go down together?'

It was not until during dinner, however, that hostilities were opened. Mrs Carlisle hadn't come down for afternoon tea and Fiona had taken herself off for a ride—much to everyone's discreet relief. And the four other guests, two couples who obviously knew Mel well, followed Sally and Peter's lead and went out of their way to make Rachel feel as welcome as possible. And then she was taken on a grand tour of the property and it was impossible not to relax a bit as the warm golden sunset turned to dusk and a stillness fell over the great paddocks and the mares and foals prepared to settle for the night.

It was Sally who followed Rachel up to her room this time after a convivial 'happy hour'.

'We do tend to dress for dinner but nothing too elaborate,' she chatted as she closed the curtains. 'Look, if there's anything you need, just tell me. Something pressed or whatever!'

'No, I'm fine, thank you.' Rachel smiled.

'Actually, I want to apologise too,' Sally Stevens confessed ruefully, and she closed the door. 'Apparently Mrs Carlisle discovered from Mel's receptionist that we'd invited him up for the weekend and she rang me this morning and—well—invited herself. Our families are such old friends, you see. What she neglected to do was tell me she was bringing Fiona, another old friend, and what I neglected to do—she did take me by surprise—was tell her Mel was bringing you, until she arrived. Of course, what Mel neglected to tell us all...' She gestured.

Rachel picked up her hairbrush and turned it over and said wryly, 'We're both in awkward positions, aren't we? And you're right. Mel is probably more at fault than his mother, but I haven't agreed to marry him, so it could all be a storm in a teacup anyway.'

Sally sat down and said with unmistakable genuineness, 'That must be such a new experience for Mel! Do you love him? Oh!' She clapped a hand to her mouth. 'Forgive me—don't answer, it's none of my business.'

Rachel said slowly, 'If you must know, at the moment I'm rather annoyed with him.'

'He honestly didn't know they were here.'

'No, I know.' Rachel shrugged, then decided to take the plunge. 'Does Fiona...love him?'

Sally grimaced. 'She shouldn't. Oh, they did have a romance years ago but ever since Mel has...not given her cause to be fostering any expectations. And what his mother refuses to recognise is that he would probably go out of his way to find someone she *didn't* approve of to marry,' Sally said with a chuckle. 'Both very strong-minded people, those two, Rachel. Rachel?'

Rachel brought her gaze back to Sally. 'Sorry.'

'Did I say something...weird? You look a little——'

'No,' Rachel said hastily. 'Look, I do appreciate you—er—welcoming me like this in these awkward circumstances.'

Sally rose and patted her arm. 'It is still our house despite the Carlisle family's propensity for sort of sweeping all before them. I'll let you get dressed—you have your own bathroom through this door.'

Rachel took a long shower and, as she was getting into the habit of, smoothed body lotion all over her skin, blow-dried her hair just as Mr Leon had demonstrated and sat down at the bathroom vanity unit in one of her aunt's ivory silk camisole tops and matching panties and a pair of white, lacy-topped, self-supporting nylons, to do her make-up. And she had to acknowledge that regular decent food as well as the attention she was now paying to herself had caused her skin to acquire a bloom and reduce the slightly gaunt look she'd arrived home from Africa with.

But it's still the same inner me, she reminded herself. How much of that does Mel see? Someone who often doesn't care how she looks and someone who had thought she'd perfected a touch-me-not technique that took the form of a cool, blue-stocking image that frightened a lot of men off. And, talking of Mel, would he really go to the absurd length of marrying just to upset his mother? No, she decided rather grimly. On the other hand he was not at all averse to using her in a war against his mother—he really lacked a lot of morals himself, she reflected, not for the first time, for someone who criticised the lack of them in others.

There was a knock on the bedroom door and it opened and closed.

'Who's that?' she called through the half-open bathroom door.

'It's me—it is I,' Mel answered. 'I brought you an aperitif; you're running a bit late.'

'But I'm not dressed,' she objected.

'Not at all?'

'Well—what is the time?'

He told her and she grimaced. She'd taken longer than she'd realised.

'What does "well" mean?' he enquired. 'Well, you are, or well, you aren't? I can see a stunning outfit laid out on the bed but no underclothes.'

Rachel gritted her teeth. 'I don't suppose it's any good asking you to go away?'

'None. Nor do we have the time for me to do more than admire you as you slip into these things, but if you haven't got *anything* on tell me where to find it and I'll hand it round the door——'

'Don't bother,' Rachel said wearily, and emerged from the bathroom. 'For someone with the background and upbringing *you've* had—a lot of it has obviously been wasted!' She strode over to the bed and picked up the wide-legged lavender trousers that lay on it and got into them.

'Here,' Mel said from behind her as she reached for the centre back zip, 'let me.'

Unfortunately she was facing the dressing-table mirror, so she could see herself reflected in it against him. He wore a pale blue shirt, navy blue tie and trousers and a grey sports jacket, and when the zip was done he straightened and looked down at the sweep of her shoulders and her bare arms; his gaze grew oddly intent and a muscle moved in his jaw.

She caught her breath, and he must have sensed it, because he lifted his eyes to hers in the mirror and it was as if there was a sudden intimate charge between them, so that every fine hair on her body stood up and she was achingly conscious of the bulk of him so close behind her. And she knew that, were he to cup her shoulders and draw her back against him, she wouldn't resist. She would in fact, she realised, like to delicately draw off the camisole top and feel his hands on her bare breasts, and she realised further, with a stunning little sense of shock, that the contrast between her nakedness and his clothes would be incredibly erotic and exciting... Perhaps I'm more like my aunt than I knew, she thought chaotically, and stepped away with an abrupt awkward movement that nearly brought her to grief—she stumbled over the shoes she'd laid out to wear.

But he caught her about the waist and turned her slowly to face him. 'Why?' he said with a frown in his eyes. 'Why the fear? The need is there—I'm damn sure. I can see it,' he said, dropping his gaze to her camisole top.

Rachel breathed raggedly and the movement caused her nipples to feel constricted beneath the silk, and he moved his hands up her sides from her waist and stroked them with his thumbs. Her eyes dilated and she shuddered slightly beneath his hands.

He said very quietly, 'Don't for one minute imagine that what's happening to you isn't happening to me.' He slid one hand up to her bare shoulder. 'Don't imagine, for instance,' he went on, 'that I'm not plagued by a desire to do this,' he slipped one fragile strap down but kept stroking her nipple, 'and that it's not going to take quite some will-power to back away from your…warmth.' Heat poured into her cheeks and what his hands were doing to her sent shock-waves of sensation through her body. 'And to back away from taking everything off you, with the exception of those sexy stockings, perhaps,' he smiled absently, 'and exploring your body.' He moved his hands lingeringly back to her waist and pulled her a fraction closer, and she breathed in the faint lemony tang of his aftershave and was excruciatingly conscious of the way his jacket outlined his broad shoulders and how small her waist felt and how he'd be able to take command of her body if he chose…

She stared up into his eyes, mesmerised, as he continued, barely audibly, 'Explore you and make you gasp and tremble when I touch you where you really want to be touched.' His hands hardened on her waist as she moved convul-sively. 'Where, incidentally, I would probably be shuddering with my own need to—enter you. And I don't think,' he dropped his hands abruptly, 'anything you've said to me so far has any bearing on it, because it's something just between you and me, Rachel. No one else, and only you and I can—resolve it.'

Rachel swayed and clasped her hands on her arms protectively. 'You said—you promised…'

'I promised not to touch you against your will. You forgot to keep your will hidden some moments ago,' he said mockingly. 'And if I didn't know better I'd be tempted to think that what's between us was not quite the—er—normal course of events for you. Here.' He reached across and picked up her blouse.

She took it after a frozen moment and buttoned herself into it with fingers that felt like all thumbs. Then she put on the wide violet suede belt and looked around for Sam's matching suede pumps.

'Ready?' He raised an eyebrow at her.

'N-no,' she stammered, slipping the shoes off suddenly. 'Mel—no, I'm not coming.'

'Yes, you are.' He caught her hand. 'Have some of this.' He picked up the drink he'd brought up.

She opened her mouth, then took it suddenly and swallowed some. 'But——'

'No buts, Rachel. Put your shoes on, there's a good girl. And remember,' he said placidly, 'that although there are times when you—want me quite desperately, there are also times when you despise me.'

'Such as now!' she said huskily. 'Yes, I'll do that.' And she tossed her head and slipped the shoes on again, but he only smiled amusedly.

CHAPTER FIVE

EVERYONE was waiting for them at the bottom of the stairs as they came down hand in hand— Mel had simply taken her hand, and his grip tightened as she hesitated and stumbled slightly.

It was Peter Stevens who came to the rescue as all heads at the bottom of the stairs turned to watch their progress, Mrs Carlisle, resplendent in topaz Thai silk, included.

He came forward with a warm smile. 'Rachel, may I take you in to dinner?'

The long mahogany table gleamed with silverware and crystal beneath a chandelier, and for most of the meal it was a very pleasant, normal dinner party. Mrs Carlisle was gracious and charming. Fiona, looking superb in a replica of a man's dinner suit complete with bow tie, appeared unperturbed by anything, and Sally— Rachel wondered if she was working overtime— was such a warm hostess that it almost hid the fact that she was also a very skilled one.

But, as the dessert was cleared and fruit and cheese placed, Mrs Carlisle said into a lull, 'Tell me, Miss Wright, what do you do with your time?'

There was a dull thud and Rachel glanced across the table to see Mel's long fingers picking up a cheese knife and their gazes caught for a moment. Should I? she wondered. Doesn't he deserve it? But she winced inwardly at the thought of the havoc he could wreak when he chose and took a steadying breath.

'I'm studying for a degree in agricultural economics, Mrs Carlisle,' she said politely.

'Really? How unusual. Do you have a burning ambition to be a farmer?' It was said with just a tinge of amazement, not enough to be downright insulting but enough to indicate that in Mrs Carlisle's estimation Rachel might as well be expressing a desire to go to the moon.

Rachel merely smiled. 'No. Agricultural economics is the study of the allocation, distribution and utilisation of the resources and commodities produced by farming. Er—what I'm particularly interested in is game farming in areas of Africa for example, where the native fauna is about the only thing resistant to the tsetse fly, which in turn has resisted eradication attempts for decades now. There are also schools of thought that believe game is less harmful to that particular environment than cattle and goats et cetera, which some people believe are turning Africa into a dust-bowl. In fact, that's the subject of the thesis I'm working on for—this degree.'

There was dead silence for about half a minute and it was hard to say who looked more surprised, Mel Carlisle or his mother, which made Rachel want to laugh, then to cry. He probably believes I learnt that off by heart, she thought.

But his mother was a quick thinker if nothing else. 'Have you ever been to Africa, Miss Wright?' she asked with gentle satire.

'Well, I was born there, Mrs Carlisle. In a flea-ridden tent, so they tell me, in Morocco. My father—well, my whole family,' she said ingenuously, 'are all—rather eccentric.'

Mrs Carlisle put her wine glass down with a slight snap. 'It would seem so! How did you meet Melville?'

'We're neighbours, Mother,' Mel said lazily.

His mother turned to him. 'Then you've only known each other for a few weeks!'

Mel lifted his glass in a silent salute to Rachel. 'It only took a few hours, as a matter of fact.'

'Oh, really?'

'Uh...Mark,' Sally said on a slightly desperate note, turning to one of the other guests, 'why don't you tell us about the new Zealand yearling sales? Mark's just come back from Auckland,' she said at large.

'Is that true?'

They were sitting side by side on a swing seat on the veranda in the aftermath of dinner.

'What?' Rachel queried.

'Having an eccentric family and being born in Morocco?' Mel said.

'Yes.'

'Curiouser and curiouser,' he murmured. 'For a moment there I quite thought you were going to enlighten my mother about Joe.'

'I was tempted,' Rachel confessed. 'I'm glad I didn't,' she added. 'I'm sure your mother believes in the pillory for that kind of offence.'

He glanced at her wryly. 'On the other hand, you were quite impressive on the subject of agricultural economics, but one doesn't generally obtain a Bachelors degree by way of thesis.'

Rachel said nothing, waiting, she realised, for him to ask her if she was further advanced. When he didn't, she shrugged slightly and said, 'I'll remember that the next time I have to discourse on my academic pretensions. Your mother is not going to let up, you know.'

'Rachel.' He paused until she looked at him, 'My mother doesn't scare you in the slightest, does she.' It was a statement, not a question.

'Assuming things were real between us, she might,' she answered obliquely.

'Certain things are very real between us.'

'They say,' she said coolly, 'when you marry a girl it's wise to check her mother out. I don't see why it shouldn't be true of sons.'

He grinned. 'God help me—we're not *that* alike.'

'But I think you do share a certain disregard for people's feelings.'

'Any disregard I've shown for your feelings has all been in a good cause.'

'Good cause!' Rachel marvelled. 'Believe it or not, I was quite happy until you walked into my life, Mel.'

'It's possible to be that way when you don't know what you're missing out on.'

Rachel sighed.

He took her hand and swung the seat gently. 'It's a magic night.'

It was. The Milky Way was splashed across the sky with a brilliance that made you feel you could reach out and catch yourself a star.

'Come for a walk with me? We won't go far in deference to your ankle.'

'Will you——?' She bit her lip.

'Behave myself? I'll try.'

Of course he didn't—but did I really expect him to? Rachel was to ask herself rather torturedly later.

They stopped at a paddock fence about ten minutes away from the house and he propped a foot against it and leant his arms on the top rail. 'Do you ride, Rachel?'

Rachel thought of the donkeys, mules and camels but very few horses she had ridden, and said, 'Only in a strictly amateur way. As a means of getting from A to B.'

He turned his head and raised a laughing eyebrow at her. 'I'll teach you, then.'

'When?'

'Tomorrow or Sunday. They don't only breed horses here, they ride 'em too.'

'And I suppose you ride as well as you do everything else, with flair,' she said softly.

'I do ride well,' he agreed gravely.

Rachel turned her back to the fence and leant against it, tilting her face to the sky. 'Is there anything you don't do well, Mel?'

He was silent for a moment, then he said abruptly, 'There's one thing I did today I—that lacked finesse.'

'I think I'll forgive you for misleading all and sundry today,' she murmured, assuming, foolishly, that that was what he meant. 'Now I've

met your mother, I can see how she might bring
out the worst in one.'

'That wasn't what I meant.'

'Oh?' Still she didn't see the trap—then she
turned her head and was staring it in the face.
'No, Mel,' she whispered, 'you promised.'

'I'm not going to touch you. I've—sworn off
kissing you against your will,' he said drily. 'But
I'd dearly love to know why it's such an im-
placable will. You know you want it, I know you
want it—and don't ask me why, but I don't believe this—this unrelentingness has anything to
do with Joe.'

'Perhaps that's what you want to believe,' she
said huskily. 'Would you ever be able to understand,' she went on slowly, 'that I value my independence above all else?'

'Oh, I'd believe it,' he said grimly. 'But the
way you've gone about it—disgusts me, if you
must know.'

'But you still want me,' Rachel said.

He laughed without humour. 'Tell me why—
at least tell me that. Did some man hurt you so
badly once?'

'No. Nothing as simple as that, Mel,' Rachel
said impatiently. 'You said you were going to
behave yourself.'

'I said I'd try. And I haven't touched you but—
all right, let's change the subject—do you ever
feel lonely?'

Rachel folded her arms and pushed her hands
under her wide sleeves. 'Sometimes,' she
admitted.

'So do I. Right now.'

'I thought we were changing the subject.'

'We could discuss it subjectively.'

Rachel moved. 'I think we ought to go back.'

'Coward,' he said softly.

For some reason that stung Rachel to the core. 'You're wrong, Mel,' she retorted. 'There's nothing cowardly about refusing to give in to a physical attraction that will lead nowhere. Look, if I were to be truly subjective about *you*, I would say that nine-tenths of your feelings are motiv- ated by the simple fact that you can't *have* me! It's the challenge, it's a typically chauvinistic in- stinct that tells you no woman should be able to dictate the terms and certainly no woman is truly capable of letting her head rule her heart or her body.'

'And if I were to be truly subjective about you, Rachel,' he said quietly, 'I would say that what attracts me to you is the way you move, your eyes, your body—your clean, elegant lines that, curiously, appeal to me far more than voluptu- ous curves—your stillness sometimes, then your fire, your obvious intelligence and a quality that I can't quite put my finger on except to say it's like an indifference to the material things Joe has given you or any I might give you . . . it's almost as if there's more to your world, much more sub- stance than a lot of women I meet. And that's really odd, isn't it? Shall we go back?'

But it was a moment before Rachel moved, a moment before she could tear her wide, stunned eyes away from him.

Saturday began slowly.

A long country breakfast was indulged in during which plans for the day were unveiled.

And Rachel heaved an inward sigh of relief as she realised the day was to be well and truly accounted for. They were to go to an annual country picnic race meeting and then on to dine and dance at a restaurant in the nearest town. To be perfectly honest she thought it all sounded rather exhausting, but hopefully would leave little opportunity to be alone with Mel.

She was wrong. Whether by design or not, she was alone with him in the Saab as the convoy moved off for the races—for the first time since his disclosures of the previous evening which had so unsettled her and even interfered with her sleep.

And, while he'd appeared perfectly normal at breakfast, he was not at all loquacious for the first ten minutes of the drive. In fact he didn't say a word.

The effect on her was odd. At first she shrugged mentally and thought, Is he really *sulking*? Then she discovered herself trying desperately to think of something to say to break the impasse.

He broke it, sardonically. 'We don't seem to have much to say to each other—do you enjoy the races, Rachel?'

She gripped her hands in her lap. 'I've never been.'

That did surprise him. He glanced at her with a frown.

'My education is sadly lacking in some respects,' she murmured. 'I—to be honest I don't know what to say to you. I...' To her surprise and horror her voice clogged up and treacherous tears threatened.

He drove on for a moment then he took a hand off the wheel and put it over hers. 'Relax.'

'I... don't usually do this,' she whispered and sniffed.

He smiled faintly and released her hands to dig into his pocket and get his handkerchief. 'Here. Use mine.'

She took it gratefully.

'How come you've never been to the races?' he said, and slid his arm along the back of her seat so that his fingers just rested on her shoulder.

'I don't know. Lack of interest, lack of m...'

'Money?'

'Well, from what I gather it can be like throwing it down a bottomless pit. I'm a bit more careful with mine than that.'

'Having a flutter can be fun, though. Shall I tell you about my system?'

'Tell me first if it's successful.'

'Now, Rachel,' he said with a grin, 'would I use an unsuccessful system? Better?' he queried as she smiled weakly.

'Yes.'

'Do you mean that's all there is to it?' Rachel said incredulously in the dusty, colourful betting-ring a couple of hours later. 'You've picked three winners in a row on the strength of what colours their jockeys were wearing.'

'Don't you believe it,' Peter said over her shoulder. 'Mel's a mean judge of horse-flesh.'

Mel looked innocent.

'I might have known,' Rachel said wryly as she looked at the notes in her hands. 'I've won a small fortune!'

'Very small,' Mel said with an odd little glance. 'Still, you could buy me a drink.' And he drew her away towards the bar.

'Having fun?' he said when he'd found them a small table on a patch of grass and as they raised their foaming glasses of beer.

'Oh, I needed that, I'm parched—yes. Thank you,' she replied.

'It's good to see you having fun—all the thanks I need, in fact.'

She was quiet for a time. Then, 'Tonight—what will it be like?'

'I suspect the party will double in size, it generally does in these parts after the races, and there'll be plenty of merriment.'

Rachel looked around. 'The landed gentry at play,' she said.

'Mmm,' he agreed.

'But not your milieu, Mel?'

'I'd go round the bend,' he said simply. 'Much as I like some of them.'

'It's...it looks as if it's Fiona's milieu,' she said, catching sight of Fiona surrounded by people.

'That's why my mother approves so much of Fiona, but—and I say this very genuinely—*I'd* drive *Fiona* round the bend.'

'She doesn't seem to appreciate that, although I think she's been terrific in the circumstances—but why is she still hoping?'

'You must have forgotten that outburst she subjected you to yesterday,' he said drily.

Rachel grimaced. 'I might have done the same in the circumstances, but why is she, Mel?'

He looked past her towards Fiona and for a moment his expression was curiously bleak. 'I don't know. It's a long time since we've had much to do with each other at all.'

For a moment Marty's face appeared before Rachel's mental eye, and she heard his words about girls flinging themselves at Mel's feet since primary school. And she said involuntarily, 'It would help if you didn't have the lot.'

He drew his gaze back to her face. 'What lot?'

'Oh, nothing,' Rachel said hastily.

'Rachel, in fact there's a lot I don't have,' he said slowly. 'I don't have a lot of time or patience, I have an extremely low tolerance threshold for fools or people I consider fools—I can be hell to live with.'

'And hell to live without,' she murmured, but before he could take issue with that his mother arrived on the scene.

'Go away, Mel, will you?' she commanded. 'I need a seat and there's not another one available for miles.'

'Mother——'

'Yes, do go away, Mel,' Rachel said, stiffening her spine and thinking, I might as well get this over and done with.

'Mrs Carlisle,' she began as Mel withdrew reluctantly and with a quizzical look in his eye, 'there is no question of my marrying Mel at the moment——'

'At the moment?' His mother raised her eyebrows.

'Well, put it this way: it hadn't even occurred to me when he—er—dropped his bombshell.'

'I see. And what do you have against him?' There was no doubting the hauteur in those grey eyes she'd bequeathed to her son.

Rachel fought a desire to laugh. 'He——' She hesitated, then shrugged. 'He's extremely arrogant, extremely used to getting his own way, he's impatient and intolerant and I think he'd be hell to live with.'

Mrs Carlisle blinked.

'Furthermore, I do come from a very ordinary background despite my family's eccentricities, and I frequently have to take part-time waitressing jobs to——' Rachel stopped and bit her lip.

'But my dear girl, your clothes alone!'

'Ah,' Rachel said, cursing herself inwardly and thinking frantically. 'Um...I do have a wealthy aunt. She—er—married—well, she married for money, you might say, someone who was a lot older than she was, and now that he's passed on she can indulge any whim that takes her. She's very kind to me from time to time.'

'Extraordinary,' Mrs Carlisle murmured in a slightly dazed way. 'Morocco, tsetse fly and now this... But——' she pulled herself together and a steely look entered her eyes '—I can't believe you don't find Melville attractive!'

'Oh, I do! It's when one comes across his total inability to bear being thwarted in any way that— one wonders, shall we say? Perhaps it has something to do with being the youngest child and only son,' she said gently.

Mrs Carlisle bridled visibly. 'How dare you? That's as good as saying I spoilt him!'

'Well, I'd be surprised if you didn't when he was very young,' Rachel said pensively. 'But I don't blame you entirely. I mean, one can't be blamed for one's genes, can one?'

'As a matter of fact, Miss Wright,' Mrs Carlisle said proudly, 'there's a lot of his father in Mel. He has his sense of humour, and if you'd ever seen him with sick children you would know there's another side to Mel...that you might never see.'

'Yes,' Rachel said slowly, with a curiously faraway look in her eyes. Then she grimaced. 'There is one problem; he's rather infatuated with me.'

'I'm sure he'll get over it,' Mrs Carlisle said, but slowly too, as if she was thinking other thoughts.

'Perhaps,' Rachel conceded. 'And perhaps I might be the right one for him after all—just say I were, Mrs Carlisle. Apart from Morocco, tsetse fly and an...unusual aunt, what would you really have against me?'

Mel's mother was silent for a long moment, then she surprised Rachel considerably by saying, 'Miss Wright—Rachel, Mel shocked me and hurt me, I can't deny it, by presenting you to me the way he did. I reacted,' she shrugged, 'like a typical, overbearing mother and a snob into the bargain. What I am, in fact, is a terribly proud mother and a widow, which is a dangerous combination but, like you, I'm not quite blind to Mel's imperfections, nor am I blind to the kind of genius that drives him. I really don't know what kind of a wife he needs, but I suspect *she'd* need to be a saint. I suspect she'd either have to devote herself to him entirely or take a very back seat. I wouldn't like to see anyone marry him who doesn't realise it.'

'But Fiona...?'

'Fiona lacks saintliness, as I'm sure she'd be prepared to tell you herself, but she is the other kind of wife who might suit him. Despite the elegant façade, give her horses, dogs, children and—well, sometimes when people have known each other for a long time, they overlook certain qualities.'

'Does Fiona—is she in love with him?'

'I think she thinks she is.'

Rachel sighed.

'That's not your fault.'

'No. No, but I feel a bit...' Rachel gestured.

'Feel a bit hot?' It was Sally who broke into the conversation. 'Me too!' She fanned herself vigorously with her race book. 'Look, I'm just about to suggest to Pete that we head off for the nearest hotel where we can all freshen up before we go to dinner. How does that sound?'

'How did you cope with the Spanish Inquisition?'

They were driving along an unmade road into a golden sunset.

'Your mother and I came to an understanding,' Rachel said carefully.

'Tell me,' Mel invited with a wry smile.

'No.' She laid her head back on the seat.

'You didn't——'

'I didn't tell her about Joe.'

'Rachel, I'll pull up here and stay until you——'

Rachel sat up exasperatedly. 'All right! I told her I wasn't the right wife for you—no, I actually told her you weren't the right husband for me, and we had a rather funny little interlude where she took exception to that but in the end we agreed...we agreed on certain things and that's all I'm telling you, Mel. Pull up if you like! I don't give a damn.'

He pulled up promptly.

Rachel closed her eyes. 'You're being childish,' she said through her teeth.

'I thought you didn't give a damn.'

'Mel!' She turned to him convulsively, but he was laughing at her.

'Sorry, just testing,' he murmured and he looked so wickedly amused, so alive that she caught her breath. He put the car in gear and drove off. 'What I'd really like to know is, having got you in a good mood earlier, why are you down in the dumps now? If it was anything my mother said, I apologise, but when I left you two together I got the impression you were—spoiling for a fight and didn't need any help from me.'

'I didn't,' she said briefly.

'Then?'

Rachel laid her head back again and sighed. 'I've got the feeling you've stirred up a hornets' nest...pointlessly. You've hurt your mother, you've hurt Fiona.' She shrugged. And what you've done to me remains to be seen, she thought.

He drove in silence for a while. 'Perhaps we need to be on our own.'

'We are on our own.'

'I mean for the rest of the evening. Then I could show you that it isn't pointless.'

Rachel smiled wearily. 'No.'

'Just—no?' he queried.

'Mmm.'

'All right.' He didn't seem at all put out.

Rachel frowned. 'Are you up to something, Mel?'

'Why do you ask?'

'Your good humour,' she said slowly, 'in——'

'Ah, that——'

'In the face of opposition,' she continued deliberately, 'is not at all like you.'

He looked at her wryly. 'I did need a break. I do have you by my side and I'll have you all day tomorrow and most of Monday.' He shrugged. 'At the moment I'm content, Rachel,' he said, and laughed at her incredulous look. 'Perhaps you don't know me as well as you think.'

But I do know you, Mel, she reassured herself as she tidied and brushed up in a hotel bedroom thoughtfully provided. And I do know that what you believe me to be has added a dimension to it—that I'd rather not think about except to find it incredible that I've gone along with it for so long. But every time I decide to tell you the truth—something happens to stop me and I get angry all over again and ... it's as if, now, I can't back down, not only because it's a protection of a kind, but a point of pride. How *can* he still believe that of me the better he gets to know me?

'But of course the real problem,' she murmured to her reflection, 'is that I *am* scared of getting involved with him, perhaps falling for him in a way I've never fallen before. Picking up the pieces was painful enough last time, painful and degrading and...all the useless things you feel when you find out that what you thought was love was all give and no take.'

'Ready, Rachel?' Sally poked her head around the door. 'We're about to leave for the restaurant. I'm afraid the party's tripled in size,' she said ruefully, 'but they're all very nice people!'

They were nice people. They were also boisterous and exuberant—all proceeds from the race day went to charity and it had been a bumper day, so this was a bumper celebration accordingly.

And for Rachel, there was never a dull moment as she was exuberantly welcomed into their midst and, after dinner, danced with until her ankle started to ache.

It was Mel who came to her rescue. The nature of the party had precluded any intimate moments, but he must have seen her stumble on the dance-floor, because he loomed up and took her away from the man who had been dancing with her and telling her at the same time and in great detail about his Simmental cattle.

'I can't dance another step, Mel.'

'I know. I thought we might go home. A lot of this mob will party on to dawn if I'm any judge. Do you feel like that?'

'No,' she said wearily. 'How do they do it? The races, the driving alone——' She shook her head.

'They don't do it that often, so they get the best mileage out of it they can. Sit here. I'll make our excuses.' He walked away looking for Sally and Peter.

Rachel sat gratefully and leant down to rub her ankle.

And in the car on the way back to Lilianvale, she fell asleep and didn't realise they'd arrived until he opened her door and lifted her into his arms.

'Oh,' she said drowsily. 'I can walk. Have I been asleep for long?'

'About twenty-five miles.'

'Sorry.' She moved her cheek against his jacket and said without thinking. 'I always dreamt of being swept off my feet and made to feel as light as feather, but you're the first man to do it.'

He didn't comment until they were inside and he was putting her down on a comfortable settee. Then he said, 'If that's true, Rachel, then I could be the first man to...do other things for you.'

Her drowsiness fled and she sat up and rubbed her eyes. 'I...what I meant...' Her shoulders slumped. 'All girls have those Cinderella fantasies,' she said rather bleakly.

'I'd just like to know,' he was standing in front of her, staring down at her and he looked tall and austere, 'what shattered your girlish fantasies so completely. Would you like a cup of coffee?' He gestured to a table where cups and biscuits were set out and a coffee percolator simmered gently.

'I—thank you,' she said, trying to gauge his mood and realising, belatedly, how alone they were. But she couldn't tell much as he poured the coffee, and with a little sigh she slipped her shoes off and rubbed her ankle again.

'Let's have a look.'

She glanced up distractedly. 'It's all right!'

He pushed a leather footstool towards her. 'It won't hurt to put it up.'

'Thanks,' she murmured, and put both her feet up gratefully. 'What I really need is a long hot bath. To wash away the dust. Thanks,' she said again as he put her coffee and a biscuit on a table beside her, and watched as he took off his jacket and tie, slung them over a chair, and sat down opposite her.

And as the silence lengthened and for Rachel, the tension grew, she found herself saying suddenly, 'I'm different, Mel. I was different as a girl and——'

'Not that different, apparently.'

'I——'

'You said yourself, most girls have their Cinderella fantasies.'

'Oh, that. Yes, well.' She shrugged. 'But it didn't take up much of my life.'

'How are you different, then, Rachel?' He sat back with his hands spread out on the arms of the chair and an expression that was oddly clinical, and it occurred to her suddenly that, if anything, *he* was different. She'd seen him laughing and in a good humour today, she'd seen him laughing and wicked at times, often she'd seen him dangerously ill-humoured, and damningly offensive—but never like this. Almost as if I were a patient, she thought with a little jump of her heartbeat, then a contraction of her nerves that warned her to be careful—but how and why? she wondered.

'Well, I'm not the embodiment of—all those womanly virtues—and before you comment,' she said drily, 'I mean the domestic skills. To be perfectly honest, they bore me silly.'

'Yet you appear to be the embodiment of certain other womanly skills.' He grimaced as if the expression offended him. 'In other words you're very good in bed; let's call a spade a spade.'

Rachel said nothing, but a little glint of anger lit her eyes before she looked away.

'Or are you?' he said then with a curious kind of disinterest, a kind of unbiased offering of an opinion that made her frown and look back at him searchingly.

'What do you mean?'

'Well, I toyed with the idea that you might be basically frigid. And that your lifestyle might be a sort of Freudian backlash.' He shrugged. 'Stranger things have happened.'

Her lips parted and her eyes widened. 'You have a very strange, twisted mind, Mel.'

'Actually, I've discounted that theory,' he went on with a slight smile, 'Well, you've made it impossible to believe, haven't you, Rachel? But there's still something I don't understand. I was watching you today and you don't have the slightest suggestion about you of anything—untoward. You appear to be a mature, intelligent, friendly person with a mind of her own. You certainly don't put out any feelers towards other women's men, and in some women, promiscuous women in other words, that's just so ingrained they can't help it. If anything, the opposite is true of you, and I can't help wondering why, when you are what you are.'

'Just say—I was on my best behaviour today?' she suggested through her teeth.

His eyes narrowed. 'Then there's the way you get—really angry sometimes when we discuss this. And *that* leads me to wonder if I'm getting too close to the truth. Such as now.'

Rachel bit her lip. 'You should confine yourself to orthopaedics, Dr Carlisle,' she said after a moment. 'You're no psychologist.'

'I am a puzzled man, though, as well as a doctor. That's why I'm searching for theories and solutions.'

'Well, just take one of your—misguided theories,' she said tartly. 'I really don't think you can judge a woman on appearances, or a man.'

'Not just appearances,' he said thoughtfully. 'Auras. Women do have them.' His lips quirked. 'I'm sure you're going to tell me men have them as well, and of course *you* might be better at judging that than I am. Then again, you might not.'

Rachel shrugged. 'But in other words, you think you're an expert on women, Mel?'

He ran a hand through his hair and grimaced. 'I've had a bit of experience. For instance, I happen to know that when one is tired but relaxed and one's skin's slightly damp, when it's quiet and dark, a man and a woman can make sweet, gentle love.'

Rachel ran a finger down the padded arm of the settee. 'I'm sure they can.'

'Why don't we?'

'Not in someone else's house. Not when they're probably all wondering if we aren't doing just that—not when it means furtive manoeuvrings afterwards.'

He smiled slightly. 'Where would you sleep with me, Rachel?'

I walked into that one, she thought. 'In the present circumstances, nowhere.' Damn, she thought. Why can't I just say never?

'I don't know if that's supposed to give me hope,' he said wryly, 'but——'

'It's not.'

'Then you phrased it badly, Rachel.'

'I know—what I meant...' But he was laughing at her.

She closed her eyes frustratedly.

'Just do me one favour,' he said quietly after a long moment. 'Tell me—not why you can't or you think you can't, but if you could, would you?'

Rachel lifted her lashes and stared at him, and for the life of her couldn't prevent her imagination from running riot. She felt the quiet darkness of Lilianvale closing around her, she imagined the great paddocks faintly silver beneath the moon; she thought of her bedroom, an oasis of gentle light in the vast darkness and Mel undressing her and running his hands over her body...

She thought of lying naked on the bed and waiting for him to come to her. She thought of showing him that she was as vulnerable to sweet, gentle love as most women and that she certainly was neither promiscuous nor frigid.

'I——' a tremor ran through her body '—I should decline to comment,' she said huskily.

'You don't have to,' he murmured. 'Your eyes were a dead giveaway.'

Rachel got up abruptly and stooped to pick up her shoes. 'You may theorise until the cows come home. I'm going to bed——'

'That wasn't theory, but it does lead me to another. Maybe no man has really set you alight yet, Rachel.'

'I wouldn't bet on it,' she retorted. 'Goodnight.'

'Just a minute.' He got up and came towards her.

'Mel, no, I'm *tired*,' she whispered, her eyes dark and uncertain.

'What do you think I'm going to do?'

'I don't *know* . . .'

He didn't attempt to touch her. He just stood before her, letting his eyes roam over her and then capturing her gaze and—and how he did it, she never knew—but the force of what she saw in those grey eyes was as powerful as the feel of his hands on her skin, his mouth on hers. It was as if they were caught in an intimate acknowledgement of each other on a mental plane that was stark and undeniable—and it took a super-human effort for her to tear her eyes away at last, and stumble away towards the stairs.

CHAPTER SIX

'How did you organise this?'

'Just asked, Rachel,' Mel replied, scanning her critically from atop a grey gelding. 'Give him a bit more rein. He's not going to bolt with you, but he's not sure at the moment whether you want him to go or stop.'

Rachel clenched her teeth and stared between a pair of chestnut ears. 'I really don't *need* riding lessons; it's an art I have no ambition to acquire, believe it or not.'

'There's no way I could teach you the finer points in a day.'

'Then why are you bothering at all?'

He grinned. 'Because it's a way of getting where no car can go—don't worry,' he added. 'I'm not planning to go bush with you, but I thought we could canter down to the creek, have a swim and then join the rest of the party for the barbecue they've planned.'

Rachel sighed. It was a beautiful, hot Sunday morning, the clear air was intoxicating—or should have been—but she felt about as invigorated as a limp rag, not to mention totally daunted at the prospect of being alone with Mel Carlisle at some distant creek with not another soul around for miles. 'All right, lead on,' she said wearily.

*   *   *

But, for once, fate came to her aid.

The creek proved to be leech-infested, the little bush flies tormenting, and there was no way their interlude could be described as romantic. In fact, when they were sitting on their towels drying off after their hasty, curtailed swim, warding off both flies and ants, Rachel began to feel quite cheerful and much more able to cope with things like the impact of Mel and his superb body in dark green swimming-trunks.

'The Australian bush at its worst,' she said with a grin. 'I don't know what you had in mind for this morning, Mel, but you couldn't have picked less—seductive surroundings.'

'Amazing, isn't it?' he agreed ruefully. 'For a man of my experience particularly. No wonder they looked at me as if I was a bit mad at the stables. However, I'm prepared to swear that I've swum in this creek over the years and the leeches are new.'

'At least we don't have to worry about getting bilharzia——' She stopped and glanced at him warily.

'Ah.' He returned her look narrowly. 'Now only someone who did know a bit about Africa would know about bilharzia,' he murmured. 'Did you encounter it the same time as you encountered the tsetse fly?'

'More or less.'

'And that's why things like leeches don't throw you into hysterics?'

'I don't like leeches,' Rachel said, 'but when you're used to checking your shoes for scorpions and wondering if you've picked up sleeping sickness or tick fever—no, they don't.'

'Are you trying to tell me this interest in agricultural economics is no dilettante's whim, Rachel?' he said softly.

She was silent for a time, sitting in her blue one-piece costume with her knees drawn up and her chin resting on them. Silent and stung. 'I have a master's degree in it,' she said at last.

She heard his indrawn breath. 'And the thesis? Is it for your doctorate?'

'Yes...'

'So what the hell's going on, Rachel?'

She shrugged and glanced at him again and read the shock plainly in his eyes, shock warring with disbelief. Then he said with a tinge of satire, 'You haven't fed me any other misinformation, by any chance, have you?'

'Mel,' she said slowly. 'I did tell you—you were the one who didn't take it seriously, but——'

'I still find it hard to,' he murmured. 'But if it's true it makes your way of life even less acceptable,' he said, and now there was raking scorn in his eyes.

Rachel gritted her teeth at the same time as she thought bitterly, He does have to be a prime example of a dyed-in the-wool typical *man*, doesn't he? Still ready to believe the worst of me but use me for his own gratification—how low can you go?

'I don't see what one's academic qualifications have to do with one's way of life. Believe me, it's no guarantee of morals. Take yourself, for example——'

'I'm not sponging off some older woman, exchanging sexual favours for a living, having cars and clothes showered on me, and living in a nightmarish recreation of——'

Rachel jumped up. 'But you're not as pure as the driven snow, either, Dr Carlisle,' she shouted at him, losing her temper completely. 'First of all you'd rather have me free, gratis and for nothing, but, since that seems out of the question, you're prepared to buy me in a limited kind of way—I get the strong impression your generosity doesn't stretch to Mercedes cars and it seems doubtful whether you'd clothe me—but you have no more intention of making an honest woman out of me than...than...what's his name!'

'Joe. That's his name,' he drawled. 'Do you get them confused from time to time, Rachel? Of course, it's not his real name, is it? But I'll tell you a point you've missed in all this: were you not a...dedicated, professional mistress, who knows what could have come out of our relationship? Even the honesty and wedding bells you carry on about from time to time——'

'If,' Rachel said through her teeth, 'you're telling me you might have married me——'

'Oh, come on, Rachel,' he said roughly, 'we're not two naïve kids! You must know as well as I do it takes a lot more *knowing* each other than we do before one starts to think in terms of marriage.' He got up and pulled on his jeans, his eyes a cold, stormy grey. 'I find your preoccupation with it rather bizarre at this stage of the proceedings,' he added.

'That's because you don't really understand how I feel about your double standards,' she flashed. 'You tell me I disgust you but you still want to sleep with me!'

'I've told you your *lifestyle* disgusts me, and do you honestly believe I'd be happy with the kind of set-up you and Joe have?'

'You told me—you *asked* me——'

'*Yes,*' he grated. 'I asked you to live with me. What was I supposed to do? Expect you to turn yourself out on the street? But I would never,' he stressed each word coldly, 'expect you to sleep with me for any other reason than that you wanted it. The last thing I would want is for you to turn yourself into the object of my desires—in fact, that would sicken me.'

Rachel's nostrils flared as he stared at her with contempt but she sought for some control. 'Mel,' she said huskily, 'believe me, you're kidding yourself. If we were to have any kind of future, you would want me to turn myself into *something* that's not me.'

'Are you saying you can't change? You don't want to even try to get away from indulging old men?'

'I *don't.*' She took a tortured breath. 'I'm saying, there are some things you don't know about and don't understand, that I can't change about myself. I'm saying, you would be the last man to be able to change them. It would be a disaster and—I just don't have the resources to cope with...how it would end. Leave me be, Mel.' She turned away shakily to pull on her clothes and she caught her horse, swung herself clumsily into the saddle and cantered off.

He caught up with her on his grey after a few minutes, but he said nothing and his face was set and angry. She shivered slightly and wondered how she was going to cope with the rest of this weekend. It didn't prove easy.

In the first place there was another welcoming committee waiting for them on the lawn beside the house where the barbecue was smoking and a long table groaned under an array of food and drink. Everyone was stretched out on loungers and a faintly dissipated air prevailed as Rachel and Mel approached, side by side.

'The rewards of clean living!' Peter said jovially, getting up and groaning. 'Why didn't we come home early like you two? What can I get you to drink, Rachel? There's a jug of Pimms, beer, wine—you name it, we've got it!'

'I don't know about clean living,' Mel said, switching his gaze to Rachel briefly but pointedly, 'but your creek needs cleaning up, old man. We were devoured by leeches.'

Fiona giggled and Rachel hoped devoutly that no one noticed the tinge of colour she'd felt come to her cheeks. 'That must have put a dampener on things,' Fiona then said, and Rachel winced inwardly as she realised the other girl was—to quote Mel—spoiling for a fight herself this morning.

She accepted a glass of Pimms and sat down between Sally and Mrs Carlisle, which was as far away from Fiona as she could get.

'Oh,' Mel raised his glass and drawled, 'it takes a lot more than a few leeches to intimidate Rachel. In fact I'd go as far as to say she is one tough lady. Here's to you, Rachel Wright,' he said softly but with patent insolence.

If it hadn't been all the other things it was, it would have been funny, and as a cure for hangovers almost miraculous, as the whole gathering took a concerted breath and sat up and displayed much more alertness than had hitherto been the case. They all also started to talk at once but it was a long moment before Rachel could tear her incredulous, angry gaze from Mel's bland, mocking one.

'Oh, dear,' Mrs Carlisle said not quite beneath her breath. 'But I don't understand. What's happened?' she asked Rachel.

'Your son,' Rachel spoke through her teeth, 'has just been thwarted, Mrs Carlisle, that's all. Don't let it bother you. It might be good for the state of his soul.'

There was a polo game scheduled for the afternoon on a neighbouring property. Rachel considered declining to go, in fact she seriously considered asking Sally if she could get her back to Sydney somehow, but Mel's mother took a surprising hand in things.

'Rachel will come with me this afternoon,' she said with some of her old imperiousness as arrangements were being discussed. 'I have a lot of space in the car.' Which indeed she did, in her Rolls-Royce Corniche. 'Mel can take Fiona,' she added, causing a further electrification of the party, although what Mel thought of it wasn't apparent beyond a narrow, searching look he cast his mother.

But there was method in her madness apparently, which she explained to Rachel as they cruised sedately along. Rachel herself was feeling somewhat shell-shocked as she sat in the big car. Mel had made no further comments, he hadn't even ignored her particularly during the barbecue lunch, but the sheer casualness of his manner spoke volumes.

'I must apologise for Melville,' Mrs Carlisle began stiffly.

'Please, you don't have to,' Rachel murmured.

'I know I don't have to! All the same, I am. I gather you've ended the affair and he hasn't taken kindly to it, although I found his allusion rather strange.'

Rachel said nothing.

'The reason I sent Fiona with him, as I explained to him,' Mrs Carlisle continued, 'was because I thought they should have the opportunity to talk privately. Fiona is a forthright person——

'I know.'

'And it's time she stated her case, and he stated his.'

'Did you also explain that to Fiona?' Rachel queried somewhat dazedly.

'Yes.'

Rachel shook her head. 'You amaze me, Mrs Carlisle.'

'To be honest, you amaze me, Rachel. I still find it hard to believe you don't want him. Er—

are you holding out for marriage?' she enquired delicately.

'No—we wouldn't suit, that's all.'

'Hmm ... Are you interested in polo?'

'Not in the slightest,' Rachel said wearily.

Mrs Carlisle chuckled. 'In lots of respects you're a girl after my own heart, Rachel. You speak your mind. Well, here we are.'

Here we are indeed, Rachel thought some time later, watching the landed gentry at play yet again. How ... did I get myself into this?

'Penny for your thoughts?' Fiona slid into the chair beside Rachel.

'I was wondering,' Rachel said slowly, 'whether I mightn't wake up and find it was all a— nightmare.'

Fiona laughed quietly. 'Mel's a ... dangerous person to cross. I'm sorry for the things I said the day you arrived.'

'No, I'm sorry for even being here,' Rachel said swiftly. 'I should never have come—not that I had any idea of the mayhem it would cause, but it was under false pretences nevertheless.'

Fiona considered. 'At least,' she said at last, 'one good thing has come of it. I've rid myself of any delusions I might have had——'

'Fiona——'

'No, Rachel,' the other girl said steadily. 'God knows who he'll marry, but it won't be me.'

'Did he ... did he ...?' Rachel couldn't get the words out.

Fiona grimaced. 'He was rather funny and quite sweet, and the way he put it was that he was quite sworn off marriage for the time being, possibly for life—I don't believe that, but I think you've made an impression on him far deeper than I ever did. Of course, he refused to be drawn when I asked him . . . about you. He handled the whole awkward thing with impeccable gallantry, including the embarrassing fact that he hasn't given me any reason to hope for years and I allowed myself to be talked into coming this weekend by his mother.' She grimaced. 'But that's exactly what made me understand, funnily enough, and really opened my eyes. He's not going to be gallant with you, Rachel. I——' she paused '—I once thought I'd give my eye-teeth to be in that position with Mel. Now I know I'm just not cut out for it.'

'I wonder who is,' Rachel said slowly, unable to suppress a slight shiver.

Fiona shrugged and glanced first to where Mel sat with his mother, deep in conversation, and then at her, unable to suppress the curiosity in her eyes.

Mel drove her back to Lilianvale after the match.

'I take it polo doesn't excite you, Rachel.'

'No,' she agreed.

'What are your leisure tastes?' he enquired.

'I don't think there's any need for us to go into that, Mel.'

'Just humour me, Rachel,' he murmured. 'We have tonight to get through and then the drive back to Sydney tomorrow.'

'Why should I humour you?' she said bitterly. 'You've turned this weekend into a nightmare for me, one way or another. Your lack of tact, your sheer bad manners, your—oh, no, it's about time people stopped humouring you, Mel.'

'Then let's discuss a curious phenomenon. My mother approves of you.'

Rachel felt like laughing. 'Your mother is not as bad as I first thought—a bit prone to meddling, as Fiona can no doubt testify, but not blind about you. She probably thinks you won't be able to make a doormat of me, and she's right, but really, I don't think she's in a position to make any further judgements on the matter.'

He drove in silence for a while. 'How long do you expect your thesis to take?'

'At the rate I'm going,' Rachel said dismally and rashly, 'a lot longer than I'd planned.'

'My apologies for being such a disruption—to your peace of mind,' he said with a wicked little smile. 'So Joe's overseas trip was a blessing in fact? How will *he* cope when you want to be beetling off to Africa to supervise game farming, I wonder? Or do you change masters to suit your study tours?'

Rachel glanced at him coldly and kept her lips firmly shut.

'I must say,' he continued meditatively, as they turned into the long Lilianvale drive, 'I'm now beginning to be curious about this eccentric family of *yours*.'

'I told you, my parents are dead.'

'What about this generous aunt of yours? Or was she just an invention to appease my mother's sensibilities?'

'No, she does exist,' Rachel said slowly.

'In the...way-out form you described her?'

'More or less. Mel, I think we've said all there is to say and you're *right*. We do have tonight to get through. I'm warning you, enough is enough. If you have any more plans to humiliate me in front of your friends and your mother, don't be surprised if I retaliate.'

His long fingers lay loose on the wheel. 'How *do* you suggest we cope with tonight, Rachel?'

'I've no idea...' She sighed and pushed her hands through her hair. 'I can't believe I came,' she said barely audibly.

He pulled the car up on the gravel forecourt and turned to her, resting an elbow on the steering-wheel. 'You came,' he said very quietly and put a finger under her chin, 'because you couldn't help yourself. Not even your unreasonable fear of me—which I haven't altogether fathomed but I will—stopped you. At least admit that much, Rachel.'

'Little to know,' her eyes glittered, 'that you can't even behave like a gentleman, but now I do and I don't admit——'

'Rachel——' his eyes flickered to her mouth down to her breasts and back to her eyes '—God knows what we're fighting about, but we're in too deep to bother with polite concepts—it's war, in case you hadn't realised it, and you're welcome to do your damnedest tonight—as I will if the mood takes me.'

She said one single desperate word. *'Why?'*

'I've told you. I want you.'

'But I still don't understand. Of all the hundreds, thousands of women you could have, why me?'

'I've told you that too.'

'Mel, if you'd seen me a couple of months ago, you wouldn't have given me a second look,' she whispered.

'Want to bet? Don't you realise, the essence of your attraction is a—touch-me-not kind of quality, and it's in your eyes, your gestures, the things you say and how you might look while you're chasing down tsetse fly—I presume that's what you mean about a couple of months ago?—can't change it. But, by all means——' he traced the line of her cheekbone with his finger '—don't give in without a fight. I'm enjoying it, for all that I'm somewhat mystified.' And he kissed her lightly on the lips. 'Just don't forget,' he said quite soberly then as she touched her fingers to her mouth involuntarily, 'that a war of words is one thing, a war of the senses quite another. They—tend to speak for themselves.' And he held her gaze with that same sober look until she coloured slightly and had to close her eyes to escape it.

Rachel lay in the bath soaking away the dust of the polo match and attempting to gird her loins for the next encounter. But she had to admit that the last part of their last encounter had seriously undermined her defences. Why? she wondered bleakly. She wasn't an inexperienced girl. And her touch-me-not technique—that had jolted her, she realised—had worked well for quite a while, but it obviously wasn't working now, and she was as much the cause of its failure as he was. She was the one who wanted to break the current of attraction between them, she was the one who was dangerously preoccupied with marriage, although not in quite the way he saw it, she was the one who had dangerous doubts that any satisfactory future could exist for them. She was the one who knew that she wasn't built to give herself lightly, and that the toll of failure was a consequence to herself he probably couldn't begin to guess at. So why *couldn't* she just walk away from Mel Carlisle...why had she come?

'I'm no better than Fiona,' she said aloud, and sat up and squeezed soapy water from her sponge. 'In fact, I'm worse. I'm living a *lie*— perhaps only the truth will help me now.' How strange, but it would be interesting to see...what difference the truth might bring. Then she lay back and grimaced. Was this the time and place for the truth? Maybe not, but tomorrow when they got home, as *soon* as they got home...

It was a simple dinner and a quiet, relaxed evening. Fiona played the piano before taking herself off to bed early, the men played poker and Mrs Carlisle brought forth an exquisite piece of petit point.

'Do you have any hobbies, Rachel?' she asked, looking at her over her bifocals.

Rachel, who had discovered after dinner that she felt as if she'd gone ten rounds in a boxing ring, smiled slightly. 'I'm not much of a needle-woman, Mrs Carlisle. Um...I like to read and listen to music, and sometimes I do a little sketching.'

Mrs Carlisle looked gratified and Rachel concluded that there was something ladylike about sketching but before she could do any more delicate probing, the poker game broke up, Sally put some music on and said laughingly to Peter, 'Come on, old thing, how about a dance?'

There were several good-natured protests and reminders that they'd danced themselves silly the night before, to which Sally replied that what they'd done the night before had been more related to tribal war dancing than anything else.

Rachel stood up and opened her mouth to say she thought she'd go to bed, but Mel loomed up beside her, read her mind accurately and took her hand, saying with a wicked little glint in his eyes, 'No, you don't. Even dedicated—fighters need some R & R.' And he swung her round to the slow beat of the music.

Of course he danced as well as he did everything else, and he was easy to follow; her gathered cream linen skirt belled out and he made her waist feel tiny beneath his hands and somehow—she didn't know if it was him or the music or both—some of the strain drained away.

They did all the old-fashioned dances: tangos, fox-trots, the cha-cha, which he had to teach her—in fact he conducted a seminar on the cha-cha and had them all doing it with much hilarity. Then he gave them a very funny solo exhibition of a clumsy Russian Cossack dancer and his mother watched from her chair, and Rachel watched from the sidelines. She watched the way he concentrated and his dark hair fell in his eyes and how, despite his khaki trousers and checked shirt, he conveyed the air of troikas and strummed an imaginary balalaika and hummed to it. She watched the dynamic, light, brilliant side of Mel Carlisle and came to a new understanding of him. It shouldn't be new, she thought, remembering what Marty had told her, and his mother, but until you'd seen all the facets of his personality for yourself you didn't really know what a complex, explosive mix it was, and then you had to wonder how hard it was to handle, not only for others but for him...

'Rachel?' He stopped in front of her to rowdy applause. 'One last dance?'

She stared into his eyes and felt her heartstrings pull, and found herself wanting to say, Come to bed, I too can dispense sweet, gentle love, or sweet, savage love for that matter... She dipped her head and murmured, 'Just one.'

It was the last dance, as the party spirit started to run down and Sally dimmed the lights and went to organise nightcaps and Mrs Carlisle put away her petit point and went quietly to bed. In fact they were the last couple on the floor, barely moving to the music; he had his arms round her and his cheek resting on her hair and she was helpless. Helpless beneath the onslaught of a tide of tenderness that stunned her, as well as the imprint of his body on hers that stirred her senses to a kind of rapture, that was going to change to a kind of torment in the lonely dark hours ahead, she knew.

It had to end, but he kept her close at his side as they sipped their Irish coffees. And it was almost as if they were separated from the others by an invisible barrier, she thought once, with a tremor. How could she break out?

He broke her out. He took her upstairs, but didn't even attempt to go into her room with her.

'Goodnight, Rachel,' he said quietly, and he touched her face briefly then turned away.

Which, of course, she thought, as she got into her room but only far enough to lean back against the closed door and hug herself to stop herself from trembling, isn't breaking me out at all, but binding me closer...

Fiona asked them for a lift into Sydney the next morning. Mrs Carlisle was going on to stay with more outback friends, and, despite Rachel's wry little feeling that it could only happen in the Carlisle family, she was grateful for Fiona's company.

They didn't stop on the way home, but after they'd dropped Fiona off Mel asked if she'd mind if he dropped into the hospital, which was between Fiona's suburb and theirs. But he then surprised her by asking if she'd like to see the children's orthopaedic ward. She hesitated, then agreed.

'This is Sister Surgical, one of them,' he introduced at the ward station. 'Sister Hayes, in fact—Miss Wright.'

'Hello!' Sister Hayes said cheerfully. She was blonde, in her late twenties and both pretty and capable-looking, with very attractive legs even in flat lace-up shoes. 'Now, Dr Carlisle, if you've come to check your babies, I've just got them settled for an afternoon rest.'

'Would I unsettle them?' he queried reproachfully.

'As no other—oh, well, perhaps they deserve a treat. Do come through, Miss Wright.'

There were seven children in the ward, ranging from two to ten, and not one of their faces didn't light up when Mel crossed the threshold. In fact it was a gay, breathless half-hour he spent with them, going from bed to bed, introducing Rachel, being given demonstrations on wobbly expertise with crutches from those who could and bringing delight to those, including the little Filipino boy, who were flat on their backs and could barely move.

'Thank you, Sister Hayes,' he said finally, and Rachel realised that at the same time he'd been meticulously checking each child's condition. She wandered down the corridor as the two professionals conferred quietly for a few minutes. Then Mel came towards her, so he didn't see the look in Sister Hayes's eyes as she watched him walking away from her, before she squared her shoulders and turned back to her station.

Another one, Rachel thought uncomfortably. Perhaps a nurse would suit him best, after all?

She said in the car, 'They're so brave, aren't they?'

He nodded.

'Do you only work with children, Mel?'

'No.'

They drove in silence for a while; she didn't want to break his obvious preoccupation, but she found herself saying, suddenly, 'It's the children that get me too. In those poor, drought-stricken countries where they don't understand the transition from subsistence farming and where politics often cause it to be horribly bungled anyway.'

He glanced at her briefly. 'Do you really care?'

'I think I must. I've spent the last ten years of my life studying it and roaming the world, and it was my father's passion anyway. He was an agronomist and I think I learnt about rotational crops and soil conservation in my cradle. Because I'm a woman, though, it's hard to spread the word in any practical kind of way.'

'Rachel, if you get your doctorate, what will you do?'

She shrugged as they turned into their street and opened her mouth to say that she would apply for consultancy jobs in departments of agriculture, but her mouth fell further open as they drew up outside his house behind a familiar dark blue Mercedes coupé.

They both stared, in fact, then he turned to her with his mouth set in a hard line as she said dazedly, 'It must be Sam.'

'So that's his real name. Not much of an improvement on Joe——'

'No——'

'Rachel, don't go in. Come away with me now,' he said harshly.

'Mel, look you don't understand, I can explain, I've been meaning to——'

'What can you explain? Nothing I don't already know,' he said sardonically and added grimly, 'I won't ask you again, Rachel.'

Her tongue seemed to trip her words up. 'It's not...look, Mel, I can't, but——'

'You mean you won't. All right.' He popped the boot open, got out and took her bag out and dumped it on the pavement. 'But I'm coming in with you—just in case he turns violent and you were deluding yourself.'

'I wasn't deluding myself,' Rachel cried, stumbling out of the car herself. 'I mean...oh, hell, Mel, Sam's not what you think...just listen to me. I know I should have told you before——'

'There's only one thing I want to hear from you, Rachel. Either you come out into the open and *tell* me you want me as much as I want you, that we affect each the same bloody way, or you might as well save your breath. Because that's the only thing that matters between us.'

Rachel swallowed. 'No,' she said hoarsely, 'it isn't.'

He stared down into her eyes, then he swore violently, swung himself back into the car and drove off with a scream of tyres.

'Darling,' a familiar voice said behind her, 'what excitement!'

Rachel turned, surveyed her glamorous aunt and said with sudden tears streaming down her cheeks, 'It's all your fault.'

CHAPTER SEVEN

'FEELING better?'

'Yes, thanks. Sorry,' Rachel said, and sat down at the breakfast-table wearily while Sam made tea. 'Of course it's not your fault at all.'

'I'd be a better judge of that if I knew what was going on,' Sam said, and added carefully, 'I could have sworn that was Mel Carlisle, you know.'

'It was,' agreed Rachel dismally.

'So he looked you up after the ball? Is that how it happened? But I didn't get the chance to introduce you.' Sam put her tea down in front of Rachel with a puzzled look. 'He must have liked what he saw.'

'He didn't—well——' she spread her hands '—and he didn't look me up precisely. He moved in next door.'

Sam opened her blue eyes wide and sat. 'So?'

'He then,' Rachel paused, 'and I can't entirely blame him, assumed I was—a very kept woman, to put it a lot more kindly than he ever did.'

Sam frowned. 'That's incredible! You of all people. Why?'

'I'll tell you,' Rachel said and proceeded to do so, at times having her aunt laughing helplessly.

'Oh, dear,' she said finally, wiping her eyes. 'Dear, oh, dear! Sorry,' she said at Rachel's weary expression, and sobered. 'Look, I can

understand how he got your back up and how
you decided to teach him a lesson—I would have
done the same in your place, only I'd have really
laid it on the line, probably. But it seems to me
things have got rather out of hand. Why don't
you just tell him the truth?'

'I was going to, this morning,' Rachel said
ruefully. 'I was trying to out there but he wouldn't
let me get a word in edgeways, and you saw how
he drove off! He can be totally impossible at
times, Sam.'

'Hmm. Have you fallen in love with him,
Rachel?' Sam asked quietly.

Rachel got up and stared out over the courtyard
for a long time. 'I don't know,' she said at last.
And when she turned and encountered her aunt's
sceptical blue gaze, she added, 'How can I know?
I could just be one in a long line of unfortunate
women whose paths he's crossed——'

'Or you could be honest with yourself, Rachel,'
Sam said softly. 'And honest enough to admit
why you kept this deception up for so long.'

Rachel stared into her eyes then she set her
teeth and sat down again. 'All right. But can you
see a future for us?'

Sam shrugged. 'I don't know Mel Carlisle that
well, although his reputation is no secret, and one
only has to look at him and listen to him to know
that he's wildly attractive. But I do know you,
and I know that you're more than good enough
for him—yes, OK,' she said as Rachel went to
speak, 'you're wary and cynical and I think that
has to be because you're very different from me—
from how I was, anyway. In other words you're

a one-man woman, but you're also a deeply intelligent one with a career that matters very much to you and appears to involve a lot of travel. Now, that is a stumbling-block to marriage with a conventional man, but you also wouldn't be *you* without it. And it seems to me you've really got him in, Rachel. Do you honestly think he's just fallen for a pretty face?'

'No,' Rachel said slowly.

'Then at least give him a chance to prove something! Darling,' Sam said with sudden intensity, 'look, who can promise you eternal happiness? But that doesn't mean to say you have to be a coward and, worse, such a pessimist. In any other circumstances you would be neither, Rachel,' she said sternly.

'That's because I can handle...most other circumstances. This—is different.'

'No, that's where you're kidding yourself. Rachel, if there's one thing I know about it's men. And you have to handle them as you handle everything else, *as* yourself and with pride. And if they can't live up to it, you're better off without those who can't. And I'll tell you something else: the rejections you've had because you're not some clichéd image of the perfect wife—you were lucky, and they'll probably rue the day, one day when they're drowning in domesticity, that they fell for the old cliché!'

Rachel couldn't help smiling faintly. 'Thanks. But tell me, why are you home? I wasn't expecting you for months.'

'I'm home,' Sam said, 'and this will really surprise you, because I met *my* match overseas and I—wait for it—am getting married again.'

'Oh, so that's——'

'Why I'm lecturing you? Partly,' Sam said wryly. 'You see, it happened to me when I thought it never could. I fell in love for the first time at close on forty. I fell in love,' she said whimsically, 'with a widower with six children ranging from eight to eighteen, who knows everything there is to know about me and doesn't seem to mind!'

'Sam,' Rachel said with a frown, 'he sounds as if he needs a mother for his kids as well as your money! Are you——?'

'He has plenty of money of his own—no, Rachel, he needs *me*. So I've come back to wind everything up here and I'm going back in a month. What are you going to do?'

'Sam, if this is all on the level I'm so happy for you, and you must tell me all about him——'

'What are you going to do, Rachel?' Sam said determinedly.

'I . . . I'll at least see him and tell him the truth! That's . . . all I *can* do.'

But it was a fortnight before that happened, because he simply didn't come home.

'But how can he do without his clothes and things?' Sam queried.

Rachel shrugged. 'Perhaps he sent for them. Perhaps, like you, he has more than one home in Sydney. Who knows?'

'Well, you know at least one hospital——'

'I'm not haunting hospitals, Sam,' Rachel said dangerously. 'I'll just keep working if I'm not in your way, until he comes.'

'You're extremely stubborn, Rachel. I still don't see why you're refusing the clothes I want to give you.'

'It was your clothes that helped get me into this mess,' Rachel said, though affectionately. 'Besides, there's nothing wrong with the ones I bought.'

Sam wrinkled her nose. 'No,' she conceded, 'but they're so few and . . . plain.'

'They're also good quality and they'll last, and I'm not into clothes at the moment; my thesis is burning to be finished.'

Indeed, while Rachel waited, it was her thesis that kept her sane because, at the same time, Sam's advice had taken hold in her mind, yet frightened her stiff.

Then he came home one night when she was alone and saw light spilling over his courtyard from an upstairs window, and when she checked the street the Saab was there.

It took her an hour to gather the courage to go in—she kept telling herself it mightn't be the time and he mightn't be alone—but in the end she could only acknowledge that she'd been down that path too many times before. And she finally went, via their mutual front doors.

He took a long time to answer her knocking and then he opened the door with obvious impatience and an arrogant, clipped, 'Yes?' and stopped abruptly.

And she found she hadn't a thing to say as she stared at him, taking in his ruffled dark hair, the marks of weariness on his face, his white shirt and dark green tie.

'Well, Rachel—to what do I owe the honour of this visit?' he said sardonically at last. 'Are you going to come in?'

She swallowed. 'Yes. I've come... to explain some things, Mel. Please—bear with me.'

He stood aside for her to precede him and murmured, 'Certainly. I think you know the way. I was in the kitchen. Or is this a more formal call?'

Rachel bit her lip and paused beside him but that was a mistake, she realised as she stared up into those mocking grey eyes and felt the close impact of him. 'No. The kitchen will be fine.'

He was eating one of his cleaning lady's casseroles; he offered her some, and when she declined he got up and opened a bottle of wine and poured them each a glass. 'Perhaps this will help. Do you mind if I finish?'

'Go ahead.' She sipped some wine thankfully and wondered how best to begin. 'Mel, this isn't easy——'

'I can imagine.'

'Well, I don't think you can, but I... lied to you. I'm not what you think I am.'

'Oh? In what particular respect?'

'There is no Joe; there never was. And Sam is short for Samantha, who is my aunt, and she owns the house. She went overseas not long after

I arrived home from Africa and very kindly...lent it to me, also the car—well, she tried to but I wouldn't accept it and that's how it came to be delivered the way it was that night. She has a sense of humour. As for the reputation the house has with the old lady across the road, she got things a little mixed-up, but my aunt——' Rachel grimaced '—well, that's her business, and she's come home a reformed person anyway.'

He'd stopped eating halfway through Rachel's monologue. 'So you're telling me you're actually a lady of unimpeachable virtue, Rachel?' he said, with an indecipherable glint in his eyes.

'Something like that. Compared to what you thought I was, at least.'

'Yet you let me go on...' he said slowly, his eyes narrowing, and she knew he was thinking back through the weeks. 'Why?' he said suddenly.

Rachel shrugged. 'You were so...' She couldn't go on.

'You did your bit.'

'Yes, I know. I don't feel too proud of it, but— I started to tell you several times, but you infuriated me all over again or...something happened,' she said awkwardly.

'Well, that explains that. So there is no deep, dark secret and I, no doubt, should be feeling very foolish indeed.' But the way he looked at her told her he didn't. Yet at the same time she couldn't tell how he did feel, though something bothered her. Then he said, 'Where do we go from here?'

Rachel picked up her glass and took another sip. 'I don't know. I...perhaps I'd better just go...'

'You don't know? You amaze me, Rachel,' he said softly. 'Is that *all* you have to say on the subject?'

'Mel——' her voice shook and she realised two things: that he was angry, but also that he was not particularly surprised by her revelations, which didn't make sense '—I told you once before that part of what you felt probably lay in——'

'The fact that I couldn't have you; my baser instincts that viewed you as fair game; my double standards—all those things we've been through time and time again? Is that what you were going to say?' he queried.

'*Yes,*' she said through her teeth. 'And——'

'Then why do you think I've been carting this around for days?' He got up and rifled through the pockets of his jacket that was slung over a counter and produced an object which he slammed down on the table in front of her. 'Open it,' he said harshly.

Rachel's lips parted. It was a black velvet box, unmistakably a ring box, and when she opened it with trembling fingers there was a diamond engagement ring sparkling fire against the black satin lining. 'So you see, Rachel,' he said when she lifted stunned eyes to his at last, 'I didn't actually need you to tell me you weren't what you claimed to be. Don't ask me why, but I was finding it harder and harder to believe—oh, I still thought there was something, I still do, but the thing is I don't give a damn what you may have been to anyone else; it's what you are to me that matters most. And if this is the only way to have you, if that's the price, so be it. What do you think of my morals now, Miss Wright?'

'I don't believe this,' she whispered, and jumped up, knocking over her wine glass in her agitation.

'But that's just it, isn't it? You accuse me of forming snap judgments—yes, I did, with some pretty hefty help from you along the way. But have you been any better? After all, at least I revised mine, whereas it would appear you still hold the unshakeable conviction that we have nowhere to go from here. And if this won't do it——' he pointed to the ring '—despite your preoccupation with the idea of marriage, what would it take to get your honesty? The *real* reason behind all this. Do tell me, Rachel, because I'm running out of ideas.'

'All right, I'll tell you!' She rounded on him, her eyes suddenly glinting blue fire. 'I may not be a whore but I'm not completely inexperienced. And my experience tells me I'll only get hurt...with you. I'm not built for casual romance—so, yes, I am preoccupied with a future of sorts——'

'Casual romance,' he broke in sardonically. 'I can't remember being less casual in my life. Do you think I go around buying engagement rings for every girl I sleep with?'

'But you *do* think that going to bed together is going to solve all our problems—it might solve yours but it won't solve mine. And now you think dangling this ring in front of me will do the same. It *won't*. There are so many things——'

'All right, all right.' He caught her wrist as she went to fling away from him and pulled round to face him. 'Let's take one thing at a time. So it's not a case of...loving someone you can't have?' His eyes probed hers narrowly. 'Put it this way: there is no other man in your life?'

Her lips trembled. 'No.'

She thought he sighed but couldn't be sure. 'Then it has to be a case of—somewhat lacking faith and trust in the opposite sex; in other words you got hurt somewhere along the line, Rachel.'

Her shoulders slumped. 'Yes, but it's still not that simple.'

'Tell me why?'

'I don't think I'm what you need, Mel.'

'It's strange,' he said, 'how many people seem to think *they* know what I need much better than I do. In point of fact, I happen to know I need you very much, Rachel.'

'Need in a way, yes,' she acknowledged, 'but——'

'Hang on,' he murmured, drawing her closer, 'let's stick to one thing at a time. Have you no needs of your own?'

Her throat hurt and her lashes sank, but she knew it would be useless to lie, and worse. 'Yes...'

He released her wrists and brought his hands up to cup her face. 'Look at me.' She lifted her lashes. 'Tell me you want me, Rachel. For...better or worse, let there at least be one truth between us.'

'I—do, Mel,' she whispered. 'But——'

'No, don't spoil it.' He brushed a finger across her mouth.

'I must,' she said huskily. 'I mean...' She paused and stared into his eyes and knew that she was partially beaten; the way her heart was beating alone told her that she couldn't, didn't want to escape him, and that it would be cowardly and curiously unworthy now, she thought, because he had made his own judgements about her after all, but... 'I mean, I'll do anything you want but—I can't just marry you like this.'

He smiled slightly. 'Are you proposing to be my mistress?'

She blushed but said, 'No. I'm not going to move in with you, but...' She stopped and closed her eyes. 'These things take time, or they should.'

'When you said you'd do anything I want——'

'Yes,' she said on a breath and squared her shoulders suddenly. 'You once told me I'd sleep with you because I actually wanted to or words to that effect—you were right,' she said barely audibly.

'Well,' his lips twisted, 'that's a start.' And he bent his head and began to kiss her.

'Bring another glass,' he said some time later, when they'd separated, both breathing unsteadily, and he picked up his glass and the bottle.

There was a lamp on in his bedroom and he closed the door behind them and leant against it for a moment, just watching her as she walked over the table under the window and stared down at the books on it unseeingly. Then she turned and stood with her arms at her side, her eyes downcast.

He pushed himself away from the door and got rid of the glass and bottle. 'You look—are you having second thoughts?'

She shook her head, but shivered slightly in her plain white cotton blouse and pale grey twill trousers.

'What is it, then?' he said very quietly, and came to stand right in front of her but not touching her.

She hesitated. 'I—haven't done this for a while,' she murmured, lifting her eyes to his at last.

She saw his breath jolt. 'I doubt if I'll take exception to that,' he said. 'I myself, on the other hand,' he added, 'am possessed of a hunger that's been exceedingly hard to control.' He grimaced and his eyes glinted with self-directed mockery. 'All the same, I think we can do this slowly. Come.' He took her hand and led her to the bed, sweeping the cover off. 'Take your shoes off.' He piled the pillows up.

She sat down then swung her legs on to the bed and leant back.

'Comfortable?' he queried.

'Mmm...' But there was still a glint of wariness in her eyes as she watched him pour more wine for them and strip his tie off, then fiddle with a compact disc player she hadn't noticed before, built into the bedside table, until Vivaldi flooded the room. He turned it down and sat down to unlace his shoes, then he handed her her glass and stretched out beside her.

'I had good news today—drink some,' he said gently, closing his hand over hers.

She sipped her wine gratefully. 'Tell me.'

'That kid I operated on—he's going to walk, not perfectly but—all the same.'

'Oh, Mel,' she said on a breath. 'I'm so pleased—for you both.'

'I'm rather pleased myself. Tell me how your thesis is going.'

She smiled wryly. 'It's going, but I feel as if I've been pushing a brick uphill...' She bit her lip.

'Good.' He smiled wickedly at her and her heart started to beat slowly and heavily when he raised her hands to his lips and kissed her knuckles, then laid it down on the bed between them. 'You know, you've never actually touched me yet of your own free will——'

'I've danced with you.'

'That's different. I've made all the running until now, but I strongly feel there should be equality in these things.'

'No, there shouldn't,' Rachel whispered, and put her glass down. 'That's how women get a bad reputation. Not to start with anyway...I need you to...hold me, first.'

He did, and he kissed her with an intensity that left her bruised and trembling, then he lifted his head and said wryly, 'I was trying to——'

'I know.' She put a finger to his lips. 'You did. *Now* it's my turn.' And she slipped her arm around his neck and moulded her body against his and gave herself up in complete surrender, thinking dimly that he might have made all the running so far, but she'd fought a battle like no other, not only against him but herself. A battle, curiously, against delight and rapture like no other, because this man did things to her no other had done. It was like a fiery torment to feel his hands on her body through her clothes and to long to be free of them. It was the feel of his shoulders beneath her hands and the strength of his legs about hers that made her yearn to offer her breasts to his hands and lips, but it was more than that. It was also the knowledge that this was Mel Carlisle, difficult and dangerous sometimes, then equally dangerously gentle; infuriating, but the man who had filled her waking thoughts for what seemed like a long time now, and had stripped her senses to this kind of abandon which she no longer had any control over. Why him? she thought, with a sudden little stab of pain. How can it be...?

But, as he eased her blouse off and opened her bra, she could only cradle his dark head to her breasts in a gesture begging him to kiss their swollen, aching peaks.

'You know, it had to come to this,' he said with an effort, later, when they were both free of their clothes and the lamplight was gilding their bodies and only the final claim remained to be made. He ran his hands over her and knelt up beside her. 'I always knew it would be—unique, from the moment I saw you in that black dress looking so proud and so irritated. I thought then that to...have you looking like this would be...'

He stopped and smiled faintly as if deriding himself. 'I can't wait any longer, Rachel.'

'Don't.' She reached up and cupped his shoulders in her palms. 'I'm ready. You've made me ready,' she said softly. 'If you left me now I'd die a little.'

'Oh, God.' He eased his body on to hers and ran his hands through her hair, then held her hard and it happened. He took her; but even although she was as ready as she'd claimed to welcome his driving need into her body, and even although she knew herself, or thought she did, nothing prepared her for the climax that came to them, for the way she moved beneath him, the things she did, the incredible unity they achieved as if their two souls became one and the last thought—that, without him now to do this to her, she would be a cold, empty vessel.

Perhaps it was an echo of that thought and a premonition of a new, naked vulnerability to this man who might not be for her that caused her to pull away from him as the heights receded, and to sit up clutching her throat and then start to stumble from the bed.

'Rachel—what the hell...?' he said roughly and pulled her back into his arms. 'Where do you think you're going?'

'I...I...' But she couldn't speak, she could only shake down the length of her body.

'Did I hurt you?'

'No! No.' She took a breath and wondered how she could ever explain.

But he didn't ask for any more explanations. He held her and stroked her hair until she was warmed and comforted, then he kissed her lightly on the lips and pulled the cover over them and turned the lamp off. And took her back in his arms. She trembled once and he stilled it and stroked her body. 'Go to sleep,' he said quietly. 'I'm here.'

She did.

In fact it was morning when she woke, and he was sitting on the side of the bed, fully dressed and shaved although his eyes were shadowed with tiredness still.

'It's all right,' he said as she sat up jerkily, her own eyes widening with something like alarm, and then pulled the cover awkwardly around her. 'You don't have to look like that and—you don't have to do that.' But he didn't pull it away.

'I—what time is it?'

'It's quite early, but I've got a long list today. One of the penalties of—dating a doctor. Are you all right?'

'Yes.' Their eyes met and held and the full reality of their lovemaking came back to her in a wash of quivering nerve-ends; she coloured as she remembered how she'd been, all she'd given and how she'd felt. She looked away suddenly.

'Rachel.' He put his hand under her chin and turned her face back, but it was a long moment before she lifted her lashes. To see him staring at her sombrely. Then his pager buzzed and his mouth hardened. 'I'm running late. Will you have dinner with me tonight?'

'H-here?' she stammered.

'No. I'll take you out to some neutral territory. And you can tell me,' he said slowly, 'what went wrong last night. But stay here and rest as long as you like. I'll pick you up at seven.' He cupped her cheek and for the life of her she couldn't help herself from turning her mouth to his wrist and kissing it. Then he was gone and a few minutes later she heard the Saab roar away.

She lay back and closed her eyes but not for long, and it was in her aunt's unique bath, that she'd once visualised sharing with Mel, where she washed her body that bore the marks of his driving passion—and wondered what she'd done to herself.

Sam didn't come home until just before seven, and she took one look at Rachel wearing a slim blue linen dress the colour of her eyes—her only extravagance in her new wardrobe, and her mother's pearls, her only jewellery—and said, 'It's happened!'

Rachel annoyed herself by blushing. 'I don't know how you can tell but—yes.'

'I can tell by your eyes that *something's* happened—darling, what——?' But the doorbell rang.

'That's him,' Rachel said, and picked up her purse. 'Forgive me, but I'm going to——'

'Oh, no, you're not. Stay where you are,' Sam commanded. 'I'm going to invite him in and offer him a drink.'

'Sam...' But Sam went with a toss of her head.

Rachel ground her teeth then followed.

'Dr Carlisle,' Sam was saying to Mel, still framed in the front doorway, 'we have met! I'm

Samantha Soldido, Rachel's aunt—I don't know if she's told you about me yet, but I believe I have to take some of the blame for certain misunderstandings that occurred between you two. Do come in!'

Mel's and Rachel's eyes met as she stepped aside and his were a wry, amused grey.

'I've explained all that, Sam,' Rachel said. 'You don't—— '

'But I'm delighted to meet your aunt, Rachel,' Mel murmured, switching his gaze back, 'Rather to meet you again, Mrs Soldido. Of course— Rachel was part of your party at the charity ball! Now that's something she didn't explain to me.'

Sam pouted then grinned impishly. 'I begged her to come to make up the numbers—I had no idea her... opposite number was going to be so smitten. It was rather funny really.' Rachel grimaced but Sam went on blithely, 'Well, so long as that's all sorted out, come and have a drink. By the way—— ' she led the way into the *salon* '— I've got something to tell you, Rachel, and I guess it will be of interest to you too, Mel—may I call you that? I've sold this house.'

CHAPTER EIGHT

'SHE'S quite a character, your aunt.'

Rachel stirred her aperitif and nodded. They hadn't said much in the car and Mel hadn't touched her at all, but then it had only been a short drive to the restaurant, where they'd been immediately ushered to a very private table.

'At least,' he said slowly, 'she filled me in about your parents. Which makes it easier to understand why you're a bit of a loner.'

'I suppose I am,' Rachel agreed, then added thoughtfully, 'Wouldn't the same be true of you, though, Mel?'

He sat back and narrowed his eyes. 'Is this anything to do with that thorny question, why we might not suit—quote unquote?' he said drily.

Rachel shrugged and stared down at the table.

'Look,' he said at last, 'I think you're going to have to tell me how it's been for you—thanks,' he murmured with a tinge of impatience, as their entrées were served. 'I mean, you seem to have lost faith to quite a degree. You made love to me last night in a way that was——'

'Don't, Mel,' she said shakily.

'To a *passionate* degree,' he said deliberately, 'that was—electrifying. Then you wanted to run away as soon as it was over. Are you always such a passionate loner, Rachel?'

Rachel fought for composure. 'If you brought me to neutral territory to insult me, hoping you'd be able to get away with it——'

'Am I insulting you?' he drawled. 'What I said can only be an insult if that's your normal *modus operandi*. If you're a love-'em-and-leave-'em type.'

'I'm *not*. You're much more likely to be one of those!'

He smiled coolly. 'I also asked you to marry me—you keep forgetting that, or refusing to take it into account. Do start,' he said politely, and picked up his oyster fork.

Rachel had ordered them too and she wondered if she could even swallow oysters. But she found she could, and that the small task of eating restored her nerves a little. 'Mel,' she said when she was finished, 'your offer of marriage was—couched in unusual terms, if you remember. You mentioned things like the price to pay et cetera, and——'

'I also said,' he returned swiftly, 'that the only thing that mattered was what you meant to me.' And his grey gaze was suddenly cutting.

The wine steward intervened at this point. Rachel picked up her glass as he departed. 'That was when you still believed I had a dark secret in my past.'

'I haven't changed my mind about that. But now I see it as a series of events—your parents virtually casting you off, some man making you feel less than adequate——'

'Two,' Rachel said. 'All right, I will tell you, Mel. I did learn to be a loner and there *were* times when it hurt, and times when you reason that you're better off just relying on yourself. But then I began to see that what drove my father was also in me, and I began to wonder how *I* would cope with a true, deep relationship. To put it simply, I didn't. I fell in love twice and both times I felt... pulled apart and—well, yes, despite what my aunt has to say on the subject,' she said ruefully, 'I ended up feeling inadequate and a few other things I don't like to recall. So I was then faced with the fact that I was even more like my father than I'd thought—not a sterile, passionless creature as I'd begun to think, but capable——' she stopped, stared at her wine, then lifted her eyes to his '—of loving—he *loved* my mother—but *incapable* of matching the other side of me up to an enduring relationship. And that's why I put up such a fight against you, Mel, and why, last night, I wanted to run away. I—you see...' She stopped and sighed.

'Go on.'

She sniffed. 'Then there's you. Of all people, I can't see how you could cope with the way I am, but even that pales besides wondering how I could cope with you.'

He ignored that. 'Is this—love again for you, Rachel?' he said quietly.

She didn't answer.

'Rachel?'

'I don't know.'

'You don't know?' he said softly. 'Did you sleep with them the way you slept with me?'

She took a breath, 'If I were to ask you that— how would you measure up what you feel, Mel?'

'Just answer me first, Rachel. Did you?'

It was a distraught breath she took this time as his grey eyes seemed to bore into her soul and there was no place to hide. 'No...' She put a hand to her mouth.

'Go on,' he said again. 'Have you ever felt quite this way before?'

'I...oh, no——'

'Then I think there's hope for us.' He put his hand over hers as it lay helplessly on the table. 'Relax—here comes our meal.'

'I still can't just *marry* you, Mel,' she said desperately.

'You keep saying that—but that offer is closed for the time being. As you also said, these things should take time—and before you get cynical, dear Rachel——' a little glint of amusement lit his eyes '—and say something else along the lines of...now you've had me you've lost interest...that is not the case as I'll be proving to you. And, indeed, I hope to be quite manageable in the process.'

He was more than manageable during the rest of their meal. He was charming and interesting and he told her more about his 'babies' and a bit about his sisters.

But in the car on the way home he fell silent, and when he pulled up he turned to her and there was no laughter in his eyes, only a question.

She trembled and gripped her hands in her lap, then nodded briefly.

'What, as a matter of interest, do you imagine the old lady across the road is thinking now?' he said as he closed the front door and took her in his arms.

Rachel's mouth curved into a faint smile as she looked up into his eyes. 'Heaven knows.'

'Any idea what I'm thinking, then?' His lips barely moved this time.

'Some,' she breathed as his hands moved on her hips, 'but you could still tell me.'

'I'm thinking that I might not make it to the bedroom, and in view of your once avowed talent for innovation you might have to take pity on me and put me out of my misery on the lounge floor.'

'That wasn't true—I'm much happier in a bed,' she said demurely.

'You're also laughing at me, and I don't think you believe me.'

'Well, yes, I do now,' she said breathlessly as he pulled her hard against him, 'but...'

He laughed silently. 'Come, then.' There were no preliminaries this time, in fact they barely got their clothes off, and their lovemaking was even more powerful so that she had not the strength to even *think* of leaving his side afterwards, let alone doing it. And he didn't attempt to hide the glint of victory in his eyes as he lay beside her with his head propped on one hand and watched her recover, with his other hand possessively on her waist before she turned blindly towards him for succour and strength. Then he held her close, and then the tenderness came and he said into her hair, 'Sorry. That was—my wounded male pride coming to the fore. You are right in some ways about me.'

A little jolt of laughter that was dangerously close to tears shook her and she buried her face in his shoulder. He eased her away and stroked her face as he stared into her eyes, then swore softly and started to kiss her with exquisite gentleness, her lips and her throat, until she relaxed completely.

Then he lay back at last with an arm still around her and fell asleep.

But Rachel lay for a long time, staring at him with her heart in her eyes.

And this time she woke just before him as the sun flooded through the curtains they'd neglected to close the night before.

'Mmm...' He stirred and reached for her before opening his eyes. 'Rachel?'

She touched his blue-shadowed jaw with her finger tips. 'Mel?'

His eyes were greyer than she'd ever seen them as his dark lashes lifted, and he just stared at her for a long moment, then closed them and buried his face against her breasts.

Her heart contracted with a tenderness of her own, and she smoothed his hair and traced the line of his neck, then her hand fell away and she sighed inwardly.

'Hey——' he lifted his head immediately '—am I not forgiven for last night?'

Despite herself, she smiled wryly. 'You are.'

'So?'

'Would you like a cup of tea?'

'I'd love a cup of tea, but——'

'It was nothing, Mel.' She pushed aside the bedclothes and got up then got straight back into bed.

'Is this your way of telling me you suddenly prefer me to tea, Rachel?' he said quizzically and with a wicked glint she knew well in his eyes.

She coloured faintly. 'It's a way of telling you I'd feel stupid getting all dressed up in my best dress to make tea.'

'Ah. Well, I wouldn't mind in the slightest if you did it as you were but—modesty becomes you,' he said gravely. 'And there are several choices. You could wear one of my shirts or my bathrobe, but you might drown in that——'

'Or you could make the tea,' she pointed out. 'I am a guest here.'

'To be perfectly honest, the thought of tea hadn't crossed my mind until you mentioned it.'

'Well——'

But he went on lazily, 'As for your being a guest here, I think we should discuss that.'

'No. Tea,' Rachel said firmly, and she got out again, marched to his wardrobe where she selected a cream shirt and started buttoning herself into it before turning—to find him laughing at her.

'Dear Rachel,' he drawled as her eyes kindled, 'I hate to destroy your illusions but even breathing fire there's something unusually erotic about you in a man's shirt with not a stitch on underneath.' And he cast aside the sheet.

'Mel,' she said on a different note, a slightly desperate one, 'stay where you are.'

He stayed, half out of bed, his body curved so she could see the long, sculpted muscles of his back and hip and thigh, and caught her breath.

He said nothing for a moment as her cheeks reddened again and her fingers fumbled, then he subsided and pulled the sheet back. 'All right— if you tell me why,' he said soberly.

'I . . . I can only take so much . . . at a time,' she blurted out and thought, God help me, but that's probably truer than he suspects.

'Rachel, come here,' he said quietly but imperatively.

She went, slowly and uncertainly and he reached for her hand but only pulled her down to sit on the side of the bed. 'About last night. I'm sorry, but it wasn't only a measure of my— vaunted pride. It was also a measure of what you do to me. But I promise you, you're quite safe this morning, not——' he smiled drily '—because I'm suddenly immune to you, but because if that's what you want, that's what you'll have.' He lifted her hand and kissed her knuckles. 'Go and make your tea.'

She made tea and toasted some muffins she found in the fridge and took it all up on a tray with two glasses of orange juice as well.

To find that he was still in bed, or rather back in bed but wearing a T-shirt and a pair of short pyjama bottoms. He made no reference to it, and they drank their tea and listened companionably to the early-morning news on the radio.

'What's on today?' he said, flicking the radio off.

She grimaced. 'More of the same for me. My thesis, in other words. How about you?'

'More of the same too—well, I'm not operating but I've got three clinics; I won't be finished until about nine-thirty tonight, but I don't start until eleven.' He lay back and crossed his arms behind his head. 'Rachel, about your being a guest.'

Rachel gathered the tray and took it to the table. Then she hesitated and glanced across at him.

'Come back to bed,' he said quietly.

She did and he just held her hand as she lay back. But she said, 'I'm not going to move in with you, Mel.'

'But your aunt's sold her house—she told us last night, remember?' he teased gently.

'I know, but there's a thirty-day settlement period. I . . . I'll stay there with her until then.'

'And then?' he queried.

She turned to him with sudden urgency. 'Could we just take things one day at a time for a while, Mel?'

She thought he sighed, but he said wryly, 'All right. It's going to complicate things, but—so be it.'

'Things . . . could always be complicated. For us,' she said quietly.

'Don't you believe it,' he replied, with a tinge of mockery, she thought, but then his eyes were laughing at her and he said, 'You've got me until about ten-thirty. What do you want to do with me?'

It amazed her, the flood of sheer sensual longing that suddenly filled her. A mixture of languor and a need to feel her skin against his, a need to feel his hands caressing her until she was soft and helpless, and needing to be touched more and more intimately... She sighed, but tried to keep it light. 'There seems to be something about you in a T-shirt and pyjama bottoms that's... irresistible.'

At about a quarter to eleven, she let herself into her aunt's house and just stood for a while leaning back against the front door, her pearls in one hand, her purse trailing in the other.

'Rachel, is that you?' Sam came downstairs and stopped abruptly. Then she smiled wryly and said rather gently, 'Come into the kitchen. You look as if you need a good strong cup of coffee or a brandy or something!

'I would say,' Sam said judiciously as she placed a mug of coffee in front of her niece, who still hadn't spoken, 'that Mel Carlisle is dynamite.'

Rachel warmed her hands on the mug and blushed.

'Darling, don't be embarrassed, Sam murmured and sat down opposite. 'We're both women and I happen to be a much more experienced one than you are. What's the problem? You look incredibly fulfilled and incredibly vulnerable all at the same time. That's rather an unusual combination. Is he... only playing with you?'

'No. I hope not,' Rachel said huskily and managed to smile. 'I'd hate to think what he could do if he got serious. No, he's...' She stopped but was suddenly overcome by an urge to confide in Sam. 'He's asked me to marry him—although he's taken that back for the time being—he's asked me to live with him; he... appears not to be at all concerned by the fact that I'd make a lousy wife and at the same time he's confessed that he can be hell to live with. And I'm petrified,' she said slowly, 'that what we feel at the moment is just too...' She stared unseeingly out of the window.

'Hot to last?' Sam suggested.

'Something like that,' Rachel agreed ruefully.

'Then just take it slow, pet,' Sam said, and, in an unusual gesture, got up and put an arm around her niece and hugged her briefly.

Rachel turned to her eagerly. 'That's what I want to do, but——' She tailed off.

'He's a hard man to say no to.' Sam smiled. 'Aren't they all? But I'm sure you can do it, and I do think you should—on one condition,' she added slowly.

Rachel looked at her enquiringly.

'Stop thinking of yourself as lousy wife-material. And don't forget, all marriages take some adjustment. Rachel, you're not afraid to love for a reason you might not have even considered, are you?'

Rachel grimaced. 'I thought I'd considered them all!'

'Because of what your parents did to you?'

'Well, yes, I had considered that. So has Mel, apparently. He called me a...a loner. But...' She shrugged. 'That's a long time ago and...I loved them for what they were, which they couldn't help.'

'All the same, despite the fact that you seemed to handle it so well, I sometimes wondered—it's hard to explain but I sometimes wondered what it was really doing to you, perhaps even making you afraid to trust without your even knowing it,' Sam said softly. 'Just bear that in mind, because I think it has a lot more to do with it than your apparent inadequacies. Well,' she said briskly, 'when are you seeing him again?'

Rachel blinked. 'I don't know. We—didn't get around to arranging anything.'

Sam grinned. 'Go upstairs and have a long bath,' she advised, 'then a long sleep. You look as if you could do with it.'

Rachel took the first bit of advice, but not the second, because she kept seeing Mel working in her mind's eye. Which caused her some trepidation as she wondered how much further he could invade her mind. And wondered whether he was thinking of her as he worked or whether he could shut out everything else.

Then she shook herself and went into the spare room and firmly closed the door. And found a kind of peace as she worked.

It was a night and a day before she saw him again. He called just as she and Sam were sitting down to dinner and Sam immediately invited him to share their meal.

'Thanks,' he said. 'I'm starving.'

He also looked tired, Rachel thought, and discovered she'd love to spend a quiet evening with him, and a quiet night. And that made her wonder if she wasn't complicating things unnecessarily.

Sam left them alone diplomatically after dinner. She went upstairs saying she deserved an early night—and that made Rachel feel even more awkward and consequently on the defensive when he said quietly, as he watched her load the dishwasher, 'This is a bit ridiculous, isn't it?'

'Is it?'

'Will you come next door?'

'I—will be giving the neighbourhood a bad name if I keep coming home at eleven o'clock in the morning.'

'Are you proposing not to sleep with me for the next month, Rachel?'

She closed the dishwasher and turned to find him watching her with a mixture of weariness and irony.

'Mel, you're out on your feet,' she said involuntarily.

He shrugged and stood up. 'I recover quickly. Am I allowed to kiss you?'

'Of course,' she said softly, and moved into his arms.

They ended up in the *salon*, sharing the settee, Rachel with her head on his shoulder, just talking as the mood took them until finally he yawned and said wryly, 'Perhaps you're right—but it's going to be cold and lonely in bed next door.'

'Invite me for the weekend,' she said impulsively. 'The last weekend you invited me for was such a traumatic affair, I think you owe me one.'

He grinned. 'All right. I'll see if I can make amends. Incidentally, a lot of people I know keep asking after you.'

Rachel looked at him quizzically.

'My mother rang me, and Marty asks after you daily.' He grimaced.

'That's two people, and one of them only once.'

'Ah, but my mother has such a loaded way of putting things, she's worth ten of 'em.'

'Your mother is very proud of you, Mel.'

'As a matter of fact, Rachel,' he said gravely, 'there is only one thing that stops me from...throwing you into my car and finding the Australian equivalent of Gretna Green right at the moment.'

'And what is that?' Rachel said slowly.

'It's the thought of you and my mother in cahoots. It's enough to give any mere male the shivers.'

Rachel started to laugh. But she wasn't laughing when he left. Because he took her in his arms and kissed her with an intensity and a thoroughness that left her shaking and had every nerve-ending in her body quivering. 'Mel...' she whispered, clutching him to stop herself from falling.

He stared down at her with a brooding sombreness she'd never seen before. Then he said abruptly, 'Do you know why I did that? I wanted to be sure that, if I was going to spend an uncomfortable night, so would you.'

She gasped. 'That's...that's...'

He smiled but it didn't reach his eyes. 'That's not very gallant? No, I suppose not. Especially when I was trying to be so manageable, but my gallantry seems to fly out of the window where you're concerned. Will you still come?'

She stared at him bewilderedly.

'For the weekend,' he said harshly.

She closed her eyes. 'Yes. Mel—has it ever been like this for you before?'

He released her then slid his fingers through her hair. 'No, thank God. It's not very comfortable, is it? It certainly appears to bring out the worst in me. Will you sleep?'

'If it's any help, probably very badly.' She bit her lip.

His lips twisted then he kissed the top of her head and was gone.

It was three days to the weekend and she didn't see him at all, for which she gave sad thanks and missed him intolerably.

'I have to say,' Sam said thoughtfully, 'this is an unusual affair—darling, you're looking thin again. Is the holding out getting tough?'

Rachel hugged herself and replied obliquely. 'I keep asking myself, why me?'

'Well, it might have something to do with the fight you're putting up, but that's not a bad thing,' Sam mused.

'I don't know.' Rachel sighed. 'I also keep asking myself how, if I feel like this now, I'm ever going to be able to say no to him. If we got married, for instance.'

'You might not want to or need to.'

'And pigs might fly,' Rachel said softly.

'A lot of good marriages have a healthy degree of aggression in them.'

Rachel looked briefly amused. 'Is that a fact?'

'There's a difference between healthy and destructive. I for one know that I enjoy a good fight and a good reunion.'

'Yes, but when Mel fights he—well, it's not necessarily Queensberry Rules.'

'Rachel, you have to bear in mind that a man wrote those for *men*, from my understanding of the matter. And men use their own rules entirely for women. But if he's fighting dirty then you have got under his skin.'

Rachel made a disgusted sound and went to get the mail with not the slightest premonition.

And she stared at the bulky airmail envelope for a long moment with a frown in her eyes until Sam asked what was wrong.

She shrugged. 'Nothing.' And slit it open. It contained a letter and an air ticket. 'Good lord,' she said as she scanned the letter. 'It's from Ali Razak. We studied together at Sydney University.'

'Go on,' Sam said as Rachel read the letter through.

'He's a Malaysian and he's now Dr Razak and he's invited me to attend an Asian conference on agricultural and economic reforms to be held in Malaysia, Kuantan to be precise, all expenses paid and,' her lips moved, '"sorry for the late notice,''' she read, '"but someone has dropped out" and he'd like me to take their place and he offers me all the help he can to get a paper together at such short notice!' She lifted her eyes to Sam's.

'Now that,' Sam said placidly, 'should really set the cat among the pigeons. Will you go?'

'I...don't know.'

Over the weekend Mel neither apologised for his behaviour at their last encounter nor alluded to it, but it was an interlude of peace and passion. They didn't set foot outside his house, it poured all weekend anyway, yet the two days flew and as an exercise in harmonious domesticity was a complete success. But then they also spent a lot of time in bed.

One thing she didn't do was tell him about the Asian conference, although she started to a couple of times and dearly wanted to share her feeling of excitement at this recognition. Perhaps it was because he didn't mention his work at all, she mused. Or perhaps she just didn't want to mar the perfection of their weekend with the kind of problem that would have to plague any life they might have together.

But on Monday morning, when she was preparing to go home, he said, as he picked out a tie and squinted at his reflection in the mirror and she came out of the shower, 'I'm flat strap this week, I'm afraid.'

'So am I.' She unwound the towel she'd wrapped herself in and stepped into her panties.

'You're not as modest as you were a week or so ago, Miss Wright,' he murmured, and handed her her bra and propped his shoulders against the wall and watched her as she put it on.

'Perhaps not,' she conceded, but reached for her blouse rather hurriedly and started to button herself into it crookedly.

He laughed softly and straightened. 'Here. You've got it all wrong.' And he unbuttoned her, then slipped the blouse off and slid his arms around her waist.

'Mel, you'll be late,' she protested.

'Tell me what you'll be so busy doing this week.' He slid one bra strap down and kissed her neck then her shoulder.

'The same . . . old thing,' she said disjointedly.

'That wouldn't,' he raised his head and his eyes were serious, 'interfere with our eating and sleeping together, Rachel, even just talking. It might even stimulate us both to—greater heights, were we able to do those things together. Believe it or not, I'm quite interested in agricultural economics—and I'd be much more manageable, I suspect.'

'I . . . I'll think about it,' she said weakly.

'Do,' he recommended and kissed her lips, and released her with a enigmatic little smile.

She thought about it all week. She thought about moving in with him, but it could only be for a short time before she took off to Malaysia. She thought about not going to Malaysia, although she'd sent an acceptance. She even thought about asking him to go with her, but time was running out. But Friday went by, then Saturday, with no word from him, and the Saab was never there during the day. Is this a taste of what living with him will be like? she wondered. I might as well be, the way I watch the street—and what did his mother say? You'd have to be prepared to 'take a very back seat'. And what had he himself said? At least we could eat and sleep together, and talk—or something like that. But when? she wondered dismally. And how could I possibly *ever* fit my life in with his.

But the Saab was there on Sunday morning and she knew she could no longer sit waiting; she would have to not only go in to see him but also take the bull by the horns.

He answered the door eventually, wearing a pair of jeans still unbuttoned at the waistband, with his hair in his eyes that were still shadowed with sleep.

And he gathered her into his arms on the doorstep and buried his face in her hair and said indistinctly, 'Sorry, but I've had a hell of a week.'

'It's all right,' she murmured, shaken with sudden remorse. 'Come in.'

'Still worried about the fate of the neighbourhood?' He lifted his head and grinned down at her. 'I should imagine they haven't enjoyed themselves so much for years.' But he took her in and led her through to the kitchen, saying, 'Coffee, I think. Have you come to tell me off for being so neglectful? I wouldn't blame you, but one of my colleagues got a virus and because he's doing me a favour I took over all his urgent tendon jobs.'

'I'll make the coffee,' she said quietly. 'You sit down.'

He sat on one chair, put his bare feet up on another and clasped his hands behind his head, and watched her move around the kitchen. 'I also,' he said eventually, 'went to ring you several times but——' he lowered his hands and shoved them into his pockets '—I knew I'd only be frustrating myself.' He shrugged. 'I guess that was selfish—sorry.'

'Mel,' she turned from the percolator, 'this may not be the best time to say this, but you don't have to apologise; that's the way things *are*—and that's the problem.'

He put his feet down and sat upright. 'Rachel, this was one week and it needn't have been like this if you could forget your... God knows what it is,' he said impatiently. 'Pride? Scruples—that doesn't seem to fit,' he said mockingly and added, 'It's strange, isn't it? You won't marry me, you won't live with me but you will sleep with me—as the object of your past disgust on account of *my* lack of scruples, I do find that strange.'

'No,' she said carefully and turned back to the coffee. 'It's—and it always has been—to do with how our lives could only clash, how we could only clash eventually, assuming we saw enough of each other.'

'All right, let's discuss that,' he drawled, 'but let's also bear in mind that were I to take you upstairs now you'd make love to me—do you know how you do it? So completely, so defencelessly I—worry about you, Rachel,' he said slowly.

She caught her breath and turned with a frown in her eyes. 'What do you mean?'

'It's hard to say. But I sometimes think of you without me and—I worry.' He shrugged. 'Perhaps you can explain it.'

She didn't even try, because she knew exactly what he meant, even if he couldn't quite define it himself; it was if the scales fell from her eyes suddenly. It was not the problem of their careers that worried her now, it wasn't her independence—she would never be able to be independent of him again, she knew—and knew the plain, stark, unbelievable irony of it was that she wanted a very conventional marriage with Mel Carlisle because she was helplessly in love with him; she never had and never could again give herself so completely to a man as she had given herself to him. Already she was counting the days and hours he spent away from her and feeling hurt because he hadn't lifted a phone. She shivered inwardly, and if she hadn't wanted to cry would have been tempted to laugh, because she'd thought she had his same ability to turn herself off from everything else but her work; she'd thought it mattered that much to her, only to find that nothing mattered but him, only to realise that she was after all just a woman who would trade everything for a kitchen sink to be tied to—and had picked perhaps the worst kind of man for that... It was that simple and that impossible.

'Mel, I'm going back overseas,' she said, and wiped away an errant tear.

He went very still. 'Just like that?'

'Yes.' The coffee perked and she poured it clumsily and had to get a cloth to wipe the counter.

'Well, well.' His eyes were hard and they never left her face as she set the mug down in front of him. 'You're full of surprises, Rachel.'

'I know I should have told you sooner,' she whispered, 'but——'

'So you've known for a while?' he shot at her.

She bit her lip. 'Not that long...'

'But while we were—last weekend, for instance?' he said softly, but his eyes glittered.

'Yes...'

'So that was to be our swansong, Rachel?'

She took an agitated breath. 'Well——'

'You really should have told me, Rachel.' He got up slowly but with a kind of menace that made her step backwards. 'Because that might have been your swansong, my dear, but it certainly wasn't mine.'

'No, Mel—what are you doing,' she gasped.

He didn't bother to explain. He simply picked her up and took her upstairs and his only comment was, 'You seem to be lighter than you were the last time I did this.'

'Don't do this, Mel,' she said shakenly. 'I don't want it, like this. Don't make me fight you and——'

He laid her down on the bed. 'Fight me?' he said softly. 'You could always try.'

She closed her eyes. 'Even if I don't fight you, which would only give you the satisfaction of proving you're stronger, it would still be...'

'Rape?' he suggested. 'I doubt it, and I'll show you why.' And he started to undress her. Then he stripped his jeans off and lowered himself lightly on to her, resting on his elbows so he could watch her face.

She tightened her mouth and pressed her arms to her sides and her legs together, which brought a glint of amusement to his eyes. Then he bent his head and began to kiss her body, and his lips moved on each nipple in turn, taking it between his teeth and tugging gently until she moved and valiantly tried to suppress a shiver of desire.

He lifted his head and watched her narrowly for a moment, then resumed his downward path of damning, shaming delight, across her flat belly and lower.

'Mel,' she breathed at last, and got her hands free to press her fingers urgently through his hair in a gesture she couldn't contain, 'oh...' And she arched her throat and her whole body quivered.

He stopped, but only to lie on his back in one swift movement, taking her with him, and to fit her hips over his to thrust deeply into her—which was the only thing in the world she wanted at that moment.

In fact all her senses were crying out for it, and she moved on him as his hands clamped her hips to him, moved and cried out herself as that strong, lovely sensation began to claim her again to the very core of being.

He rolled her away finally, still breathing erratically as she was, but he said, removing his hands from her and any other contact, 'Now talk to me about rape, Rachel. You know——' he drew one long finger down between her breasts towards her navel '—I can't help wondering whether the deception you practised for the first few weeks of our acquaintance was not a subliminal manifestation of those kinds of desires. You are—very, very sensual.'

Her eyes widened with shock as she saw the cool, mocking glint in his, then she moved convulsively and slipped off the bed and stumbled into her clothes.

He made no attempt to stop her. And when she was dressed he turned on to his stomach and slid his arms beneath the pillow, and closed his eyes.

She stared, then turned away and left.

CHAPTER NINE

A MONTH later, Rachel got off the bus from Kuantan at the beach of Teluk Chempedak and wandered over to the Pattaya restaurant where one could sit on the veranda with a cool drink and look out over the sparkling waters of the South China Sea and watch the people of Kuantan at play. There were Malay Muslim women in their pastel, always long-sleeved dresses, worn with trousers and spotless head coverings; there were adorable Chinese children, Indians and sunburnt foreigners from the two resorts along the beach, attracted like bees to the Balai Karyneka where all the local handcrafts—panandus basketry, batik, songket et cetera from the state of Pahang—were displayed and sold.

Across the road was the Kuantan Hyatt, a gracious resort hotel right on the beach, where she'd spent the last week at the conference and had one night left before she flew first to Kuala Lumpur then back to Australia. And before the conference, thanks to the good offices of her friend, she'd spent a fortnight traversing Malaysia from Kota Bahru to Johore, the highlands, the coasts, closely observing the country's agriculture. She'd seen tea plantations, vegetable and flower farms, even butterfly farms, and always, nearly everywhere, palm oil and rubber plantations. And she'd gathered enough material to

175

present a paper contrasting Malaysian conditions with Australian.

It had been well received, and it had been a pleasant week—why would it not be, with the facilities of a first-class hotel at her disposal, a beautiful beach and stimulating company? But the truth was, she was exhausted. Exhausted and still hurting unbelievably from the catastrophic ending to her 'unusual' affair with Mel Carlisle.

She'd left her aunt's house that same day and refused to tell her aunt where she was going, saying only that she'd be in touch and, with tears in her eyes, wishing her all the luck in the world in her new marriage.

She'd spent the week in a cheap motel working on her thesis as if her life depended on it—indeed, she'd finished it. And now, she thought, as she sipped her orange and pineapple drink, she was due to go back with a suntan herself, and a heart that she suspected was broken. It certainly felt like lead, she mused with a grimace.

The sun set as she was thinking these painful thoughts, and with reluctance she gathered up her few purchases and went over to the Hyatt.

The fairy-lights in the bushes came on as she walked up the drive, and there was a party of voluble Italian tourists in the foyer taking each other's pictures in front of the central beaten-copper urn that was filled with orchids. It was their last night too, she knew, and they were off to liven up Sarawak.

'Ah, Miss Wright.' The manager came up behind her as she collected her key. 'Did you enjoy your little trip to Kuantan?'

'Very much, thank you, Mr Chang. Indeed, I'll be very sorry to leave you all tomorrow.'

'We'll be sorry to lose you, Miss Wright. Incidentally, there's a gentlemen looking for you——'

'Oh, that'll be Dr Razak to say goodbye!'

'A doctor, yes, Miss Wright, but—ah! Here he is.'

Rachel turned and it was Mel walking across the foyer towards them. Mel in khaki trousers and an open-necked shirt with a lightweight jacket slung over his shoulder, Mel with his dark hair flopping on his forehead, moving with that easy, animal grace and every woman in the place turning to look as he passed.

She blinked, wondering if she was hallucinating, but then he was right up to them and all the colour drained from her face as he said easily, 'So you've found her, Mr Chang—much obliged.'

'A pleasure, Dr Carlisle. I've made your reservations at Hugo's for eight o'clock.' Mr Chang turned away.

'Thanks. How are you, Rachel?'

But Rachel couldn't speak. In fact her legs felt as if they wouldn't hold her up, and he took her hand. 'Don't look like that,' he said barely audibly.

'I . . .' But no more words would come and he scanned her pale face and trembling lips and said, 'Let's get out of here.'

His room was on the fourth floor, one of the best of course and part of the Regency Club. And, although she desperately didn't want to go with him, she was, she found, in no condition to do anything else. When, standing in the middle of his room as he closed the door and opened the louvred veranda doors and turned towards her, she said raggedly, 'No, Mel, don't touch me,' she started to shake as if she had a fever.

He watched her narrowly for a long moment, then he said, 'Sit down. I'll get you a drink.'

She sat and lifted her eyes to the ceiling and took some deep, deep breaths, fixing her eyes on the little arrow on the ceiling that pointed the direction of Mecca—anything to steady herself, to break this unbelievable bout of nerves and heaven knew what else the sight of him had done to her.

'Here.' He put a glass of brandy into her hand and closed his fingers round hers as the liquid bobbled and splashed.

'Th-thanks,' she stammered.

'Drink it.'

She did, her teeth chattering against the glass, and as the neat spirit slid down her throat she coughed and her eyes watered, then she felt herself calming. She took another sip and a long breath, then put the glass on the table. 'Sorry. I don't know what got into me.' Which was a ridiculous thing to say, of course, but there was no amused response in his grey eyes as they rested on her—indeed, she thought with the echo of a shiver that she'd never seen them so sombre.

And they stared at each other for a long, painful moment before she said huskily, 'Why are you here? Or is it an amazing coincidence...no, I suppose it couldn't be.'

'No. Your aunt told me where you were before she left. I'm here——' he paused '—because I found I couldn't live without you.'

She exhaled unsteadily and felt tears prick her eyelids, but she refused to let them fall. 'What you need is a court jester, Mel. Someone you can insult and they'll always come up smiling, or perhaps you need a professional, perhaps you too have subliminal leanings, because I really think only *paid* women would put up with your brand of offensiveness.'

His lips twisted. '*Touché.* The odd thing is, I've never had the urge with other women to be as offensive as I was to you. And that has to mean something—I'm not saying it excuses it.' He grimaced. 'I'm not saying anything very well at all, am I? But you know, you loved me and you moved me as no other woman has, as I thought I moved you—but you left. Tell me one thing. How have you felt since you left?'

She reached into her pocket for a hanky and blew her nose. 'That's my affair.'

'Do you know how you look?' he said quietly after a moment. 'You look ... all eyes. You look thin and haunted, your hair is growing unevenly and your nails are short and you're not exactly wearing *haute couture*—and it doesn't make one iota of a difference to how I feel—to how much I want you.'

'It must, it should,' she whispered. '*You* don't ...' She bit her lip.

'I'm only better at hiding it.' He smiled drily. 'The truth is, if you thought I was offensive to you, it's now become a habit. Even my mother told me the last time she spoke to me that I was a bastard of the first order—her exact words.'

Rachel crumpled her hanky into a ball and stared at it blindly. 'Mel——'

'No, let me finish—let me at least state my case.' He'd been leaning against a wall, but he sat down opposite her and took a mouthful of her brandy with a rather wry look. 'Rachel, just about every woman I've known has wanted one thing from me—a ring on the finger. And that's had more to do with . . . what I have than what I am, but I've never seen how it could work—in fact, we had the same problem,' he said rather drily. 'I just couldn't see how a conventional marriage was going to work for me. Yet, with you, the opposite happened. And even when I offered you marriage—as a trade, and, yes, I have to be honest, in a certain amount of anger and disgust—I still did it because——' he paused again and moved his shoulders restlessly '—there was something inevitable about it. I just couldn't visualise letting you go. I still can't; that's why I'm here. And what I'm saying, Rachel, is that if I'd wanted a wife who was prepared to tie herself to the kitchen sink and wait on me and . . . feel hurt and deserted every time I wasn't there for her, I could have had dozens of those.' He grimaced.

Despite herself, Rachel couldn't help smiling faintly, even despite the awful irony of his words, because of course it was only the truth. And, she mused, despite what *he* might like to think, it was as much to do with what he was as what he had.

'On the other hand,' he went on, 'don't you think because we're similar in a lot of respects, each dedicated to awkward jobs, we could at least understand each other's problems and work out a way to deal with them?'

She sighed and stared at her hands, then lifted her eyes to his. 'Mel, there's one thing you don't know. I'm...I've discovered I'm not much different from all the other women you've had. I...would also feel hurt and deserted every time you weren't there for me. I'm——' her voice sank '—as conventional as the rest of them. I didn't think I was, but...' She shrugged and blinked back more tears.

He stared at her. 'Are you saying...?'

She stood up awkwardly and turned away, but he was right behind her. '*Rachel*. Tell me.' He swung her round and his eyes were hard and demanding.

'What can I tell you that you don't already know?' she whispered. 'You told me yourself—you worried about me. You were right to, because without you I'm——' She broke off and bit her lip. 'But that's the kind of burden you've been avoiding for years, Mel, you just said so yourself.'

He swore and gripped her shoulders. 'What I said was—you seemed to be convinced it couldn't work for us because of our lifestyles, because of how much your independence meant to you—*that's* why I said it, but this...'

She winced as his fingers dug into her flesh. 'This is worse—don't you see?'

'No,' he said, quite differently from the way she'd expected, with no impatience now, no mockery, but gently. 'Oh, no. If you're telling me you love me, if you're baring your heart at last, Rachel, then that puts a different complexion on things all together, and I think you'd better tell me more.' He lifted his hands to cup her face.

She trembled. 'But you knew...'

His lips twisted. 'I hoped—yes, I told myself it had to be, but when you left——' he brushed her tears away with his thumbs '—all the old doubts and...bloody uncertainties that have become a way of life for me since I met you, Rachel, came back to plague me. But, you see, I happen to be very much in love with you, my dear, and the fact of the matter is—let's now be entirely honest—when you're not there for *me*, nothing else works. If you'd told me I'd ever get bored mending bones, I'd never have believed you, but I have. You did once say to me something about...being hell to live without. That's what it's been, a living hell, and if two people find it's such hell to be apart, there's got to be a way they can be together. Tell me it wasn't so for you.'

She tried to speak, but it was impossible again.

'You know,' he said at last, 'I think you're judging me on false premises. You've told me you turned out to be something you didn't believe you were. Why shouldn't it happen for me? Why shouldn't it be that this thing between us has taken us both and...fused our hearts in such a way that neither of us will ever be the same again?'

'Oh, Mel,' she said despairingly, 'have you no idea how you—hurt me?'

He drew her into his arms suddenly. 'Yes, but don't *you* see, it's always the thought of losing you that does it?' And he stared down into the drenched blue of her eyes. 'Rachel,' he said, barely audibly then, 'there might be some things about me that never will change, but consider this if nothing else: I wanted you when I thought you were a whore, I wanted you more than ever when I'd had you—nothing changes it. The plain simple fact is that I fell in love with you virtually from the moment I laid eyes on you. Do you think I make a habit of... this?' He asked with just a hint of his former arrogance.

The faintest suggestion of a smile trembled at the corners of her mouth. 'No. Far from it. What are we going to do?'

The tension eased slightly in his eyes. 'Something I said has got through. Which bit?'

This time she did smile through her tears. 'I think it was the bit about getting bored with mending bones. That—seemed to me to be a true test.'

He grimaced but said, 'Then—are you telling me at last that you believe I love you?'

She could feel the warmth of his body against her own, and the beating of his heart, and she closed her eyes suddenly and laid her head on his shoulder, feeling the surge of relief in his muscles that told its own tale. 'Yes,' she said softly. 'Mind you, I also believe you'll bully me shamefully and make my life a perfect misery at times, but——'

she shrugged then started to tremble, and said with a shuddering little sigh '—I love you too.'

He simply held her hard against him for a long time, then they separated and stared deep into each other's eyes. 'You said, just now—what will we do? It's up to you. I've taken a sabbatical—that's one reason why I was working so hard. I thought we might be able to devote ourselves to all those out-of-the-way places where they need agricultural economists and orthopaedics at the same time. Have you ever thought that we could make quite a team ministering to those in need in one way or another?'

She caught her breath. 'A whole year? What if...?' She stopped abruptly.

'I told you—without you, it just wasn't working. I was seriously considering spending a year in an ashram or something,' he said gravely.

'You...are you serious, Mel?'

'Never more so.'

'Oh, God—now I feel terrible.'

'Good,' he said with his old wicked glint, but taking her hand. 'I'd hate to think all the agony's been on my side.'

That brought tears to her eyes again. 'Hey,' he said softly, 'it's over—how can I prove it?'

But, of course, he didn't have to be told.

And it wasn't until they were lying in bed, sated and drowsy and holding hands, that he said wryly, 'You know I swore once that I'd never ask you to marry me again.'

Rachel moved her cheek on his shoulder. 'There is a way around that.'

'Oh?'

'Mmm. I could ask you.'

'Why don't you?'' He caressed her back and her hips.

'I'd have to be very sure you'd say yes.'

'What makes you think I wouldn't?' His hand slid back up into her hair.

'Mel,' she tilted her face back, 'will you marry me?'

'Considering that I'm already suffering from—withdrawal symptoms, Miss Wright, I think I'll have to,' he said gravely.

'Oh! That's not very gallant,' she protested.

'I thought we'd already decided I personified a lack of gallantry,' he teased. 'However, in my own defence I have to say my body worships you, whatever else I lack.'

'I can see that I shall have to ask you that question again in a more...appropriate... setting,' Rachel said seriously.

He grinned and kissed her nose but said simply, 'There is none.'

'When you can answer,' she persevered, 'that it would be a marriage of minds as well as...' She stopped as he took her hand guided it down his body.

'This?' he queried wickedly.

She took a breath but said, 'You're impossible, Mel!' Although she was also trying not to laugh.

'All right,' he conceded. 'How about this? Yes, I will marry you, Rachel, because I love you in every way there is.' And he pulled her close and kissed her thoroughly. 'Believe it, my love. In fact I'll prove it to you—I'll take you to dinner, I was planning to anyway—instead.'

'Instead of—this?' she queried.

'Mmm. Of course I'll have to have a cold shower...'

'I've got a better idea. Let's have dinner here, later,' she said softly.

'Rachel.' He laughed down at her but with love in his eyes. 'I thought we were trying to prove this was a mental as well as a physical relationship.'

'Oh, there'll be plenty of time for that,' she replied tranquilly. 'Call them and cancel those reservations.'

He did. And it was while they were having dinner in his room much later that he said, 'You do realise that I plan to marry you with great ceremony?'

Rachel hesitated and raised an eyebrow at him.

'Also great haste,' he added.

'Can the two things go together?' she asked wryly. 'I mean, I'm in favour of the haste, but I don't know about the ceremony.'

'They certainly can—you've never seen my mother in top gear.'

She laughed. 'Why ceremony, though, Mel?'

'Because I want to show the world that I've finally captured you, and I also want them to be as stunned as I am. Simple.' A smile lurked in his eyes.

'You always were a chauvinist at heart,' she murmured. 'Well, in fact I do have to go back to Sydney for one ceremony, so I guess I could make it two.'

His eyes narrowed. 'Your doctorate?'

She nodded rather ruefully. 'I got the news yesterday and it didn't mean a damn thing.'

'Congratulations,' He took her in his arms. 'Do you know, I feel like Joe.' A little glint lit his eyes.

Her eyes widened.

'I certainly perceive it as rather a cachet to have an intellectual—wife.'

She relaxed. 'You had me worried for a moment.'

'I just thought he deserved one last, parting reference before we laid him to rest. I often felt an affinity with him, you see, when I was less than rational about you, only I decided that if I had you I'd make you even more of a prisoner than he had.'

'After everything you said!'

'I know,' he agreed. 'See what you've brought me to?'

'What?' she asked, her lips curving.

'Something very tame—a proud, besotted prospective bridegroom.'

'I think I'll believe the tame bit when I see it!' She slipped her arms around his neck. 'I have to confess that I once—well, you know that bathroom of Sam's?'

'I do. I believe I even made passing reference to it and incensed you in the process.'

'The reason you incensed me,' she said very softly, 'was because you conjured up a very erotic image of...us sharing the bath.'

'I did?'

'You did. That's why I got so cross and embarrassed. In fact, there were several times when you made me wonder...' She started to colour delicately.

'Go on.' His eyes were intent.

'About myself.'

'Do you know what I'm going to have to do, right this moment?' he said very seriously.

'What?' she whispered.

'Contact Mr Chang and have him move us to a room with a spa bath and—of course, a dining-room table, they must have one of those!'

'Mel——'

'Rachel?' But he relented and started to kiss her hungrily, saying, 'Don't wonder any more. I thoroughly approve. And don't leave me again, Rachel. Apart from anything else——' his eyes glinted '—you've ruined me for any other woman. Love me?'

She trembled as his eyes changed and became searching and serious. 'Oh, yes.'

MEN MADE IN AMERICA

Fifty red-blooded, white-hot, true-blue hunks
from every State in the Union!

Look for MEN MADE IN AMERICA! Written by some
of our most poplar authors, these stories feature fifty of
the strongest, sexiest men, each from a different state in
the union!

Two titles available every other month at your favorite
retail outlet.

In November, look for:

STRAIGHT FROM THE HEART by Barbara Delinsky
(Connecticut)
AUTHOR'S CHOICE by Elizabeth August (Delaware)

In January, look for:

DREAM COME TRUE by Ann Major (Florida)
WAY OF THE WILLOW by Linda Shaw (Georgia)

You won't be able to resist MEN MADE IN AMERICA!